Painted Cats

Painted Cats

United States of America

OSAAT Entertainment

All rights reserved.

No part of this book may be reproduced or transmitted in any form or by any means, graphic, electronic, or mechanical, to include photocopying, recording, taping, or by any information storage retrieval system, without the written permission of the publisher.

First Edition.
To Contact the Author
Email: rycj@osaatentertainment.com

Copyright © 2020 RYCJ, Painted cats. Fiction
Cover Design and Photo by Rhonda Y.C. Johnson

Library of Congress Control Number: 2020945539
ISBN: 978-1-9409940-5-5

Printed in the United States of America

for the Girls

It might be a pain in the ass getting old, but sure is a privilege for those thanking God for the uninterrupted ride.

~ One of the Girls.

Now this woman, Mother, was a real pot stirrer. She could get stuff stirred real quick, just humming one of her favorite songs, especially one of her spiritual holy ghost hymns, like the ones that included the catch phrase 'I got a feeling.' And don't let her get to so-called joking, like somebody show up at a meeting a little late. First words out of her mouth would be asking if they just robbed a bank, or had stopped by a lover's house to drop off a cherry pie. That was an inside joke.

The thing was, few paid Mother much mind. She'd been like this forever. A harmless busy body often viewed more a Shero than menace. In fact, she was the early version of the home camera. In the early days, before people, both black and white started fleeing their hoods, and often city altogether, not one crook managed to rob a house and get off Scott free. And many can also thank Mother that there had not been one case of infidelity in the neighborhood.

Well, then again, there were a few cases, alas the inside joke about the cherry pie. But that's all besides the point. Water under a bridge. Dams that burst and were no more. Nobody was talking about that stuff no more. Women started burning their bras, pounding pavements and getting jobs. In fact, by Y2K, more women chased men around desks than vice versa. Poor bastards. What monsters they created.

Point was, the women who remained on Gorgas Lane, and a few who got away, respected Mother. She married. Had children. Cooked meals and worked as hard in the home as when she too joined the workforce. All of the girls who stayed friends, faced the same triumphs and tribulations.

Like their children, they would see themselves age... and their neighborhood change, and yes too... occasionally they'd lose a spouse or two, and for a host of reasons. One of the main reasons was because it was the 21st century. Between death and women and men hating each other's guts about summed up the majority of the reasons. And still, the girls stuck it out. They hung in there. Weathered storms. And got through the through, in part due to Mother...where no man, woman or child within eyesight of her eight windows dared to willingly give her one thing to talk about.

And then came Mug's call.

"Mother, when's the last time you've seen Shugga?"

Right away Mother's antennas shot up. Both of them. Her eyes opened wide as she thought back.

"Chile, I haven't seen Shugga since Brother Thomas took over the treasury."

Mother was talking about Deacon Thomas who was about 99-years-old, couldn't count, and could barely see, taking over the treasury after another deacon with less eyesight than him messed up the books. Everybody in the church was mad about that appointment, none more so than Shugga.

"That's what I thought," Mug said. She was there when the announcement was made. She laughed the hardest, tickled about Shugga storming out of church.

"Chile, I'm surprised Shugga didn't cut up all four of your tires, with you laughing at her the way you did," Mother chuckled.

Not Shugga. At 69½ Shugga wasn't like that. Actually she wasn't like that at 29 or 39 either. She was a pain in the butt for sure... loud, talkative and knew more than most, especially when it came to church, being one out of very few who read the Bible from Genesis to Revelation, but she didn't have a violent bone in her body. She was more fluff than fold. While arguing with her was pointless, few able to get a word in edgewise, she neither used God's name in vain, nor raised the sword.

"Well, I've been calling her all week," Mug said. "I even went over there, but Doubtfire said she hadn't seen Shugga all week."

"Ump..." Mother huffed, her mental radar about to go haywire. Sometimes her mind worked like a cellphone tower when her thoughts criss-crossed. First of all, the neighbor's name wasn't Doubtfire, but rather Mrs. Dubois. And secondly, Shugga still worked. She wouldn't have left a job she talked up a storm about. At 4, 5, and 6 in the morning she still got up and washed windows ...and this would be windows at the skyscraper level. When she told people she worked for Comcast, this was what she meant. The arc of her day was getting up on scaffolds and washing windows bigger and dirtier than the muscular tatted up men she worked alongside.

"It definitely doesn't sound right that old woman hasn't seen anything," Mother went on. Aside from herself, which was not a part of her skepticism, nobody was nosier and busier than Mrs. Dubois.

One time when they were all visiting Shugga for a fourth of July cookout that old woman called the law on her son because she thought he was smoking a refer. He wasn't. Oh good heavens he would never have done such a thing around the girls, women who not only raised him from birth, but who were God-fearing and church-going, and who she herself raised that way.

But he was high. Police drug tested her boy on the spot, even though he was not behind the wheel, and found marijuana in his system. What test kit they used or how they accomplished this, nobody knew. But they did know Mrs. Dubois had eyesight of the ESP range, and that she also had a son-in-law who was chief of police. They found this out when Shugga first moved to the neighborhood, trying to escape the Johnson's to be with the Joneses. The old woman called the law on her too, all because her car tags had expired by two days.

"That's what I was thinking," Mug replied. "Doubtfire don't miss nothing!"

"Ump..." Mother huffed again. "It figures. She probably waitin' on the neighborhood to first start smellin' up to a high heaven before callin' that son-in-law of hers!"

"Oh, Shugga probably just being ornery," Mug decided, sounding concerned, but not frantic. "I might call Shirley, but really don't—"

"—Shirley's in London," Mother interrupted, the cell-phone towers in her head going nuts by the frazzled pitch of her voice. "Someone needs to do a welfare check because ain't a thing Shirley can do that far away!"

"I'll see if Deb will run me by Shugga's job tomorrow," Mug quickly offered, trying to put a lid on a pot Mother had no qualms stirring. "Them guys she works with will probably know if something is wrong."

2.

Yeah, maybe. Except Mother was thinking of something more immediate. Shugga could have fallen and was still trying to get up. Or someone could have managed to tie her up and taped her mouth shut. It was a good stretch of the imagination, but the fact was, Shugga was 69. Despite how hard she worked to prove she was fit to outlast them all, every time a funeral rolled around, she sat in the same pew with the rest of them.

The second Mother got off the phone with Mug, she got right on the line with Vera. Nobody worked faster at tracking people down. The woman should've went to work for the FBI, or how about, the CIA.

Gossip during the latter half of 2001 was had Vera been on the force, there never would've been a 9/11 and certainly wouldn't have taken a decade to find one man. This was a mover and shaker who didn't bull-jive around. She even found her now deceased first husband, who once tried to skip off with two-hundred thousand dollars of her hard-earned money. She tracked him down in an Amazon jungle. Everyone still laughed about that incident. Few words describe what that man must've looked like when he looked up and saw Vera dressed in the goulashes and Safari hat. She said all the color drained from his face. And she never heard a man beg so hard for his life.

"Did you hear Shugga is missing," Mother exclaimed like it was a bonafide fact.

"Missing," Vera shrieked. "Who would take Shugga?" she asked in her customary cute sappy sexy drawl.

"I didn't say nobody took her," Mother fussed. "I'm saying she hasn't been seen in weeks. Mug has been calling her all week. She went over there today and couldn't get in."

"Oh dear," Vera sighed. She was another one who moved off Gorgas Lane. Forget Shugga. She hadn't seen the girls, which included Mother, in weeks herself. "Has Shirley called police?"

"Shirley is in London," Mother replied. "You know her daughter just gave birth to triplets."

"Really," Vera whined, turning two syllables into a song.

"Yeah, she left a couple of weeks ago," Mother added. "Mug said she was going to try and stop by tomorrow, but you know how Mug is..."

"No, how is Mug," Vera asked.

"The same," Mother snapped. "Still waiting on one of them kids of hers to take her everywhere she go."

It was Vera's turn to "ump," probably thinking, 'why call her?'

"I know you don't fool around with Shugga," Mother continued...and like really, who did? Shugga was way out there in terms of hangability. Aside from working on scaffolds with a bunch of skull bone men, she lived in a hilly town next door to civil war lily white women, and read the Bible when she wasn't playing bingo, or sharing her knowledge with people who could care less.

"But," Mother went on, "I only know of one person who can find anyone in a hell of a hurry!"

"Ieeeeeeek," Vera squealed. "Mother, you are something else! You know that's right," she laughed. "Don't nobody's GPS work like Vera's GPS," she joked, picking lint off her pink cashmere sweater with her pretty manicured nails. They were recently done. Almost matched the color of her sweater, and the flushed complexions of two men sitting across from her in the service department where she was having the oil changed in her sporty c-class white Benz.

"Look, I'll run by Shugga's and check on her," she told Mother. "I'm sure it's nothing. She's probably in there reading her Bible," she chuckled. "I'll give you a ring...or tell Shugga to call you."

3.

Vera rolled up to Shugga's modest townhome and hopped out of her sporty white Benz. Her hair was teased way up there on top of her head. Long Shirley Temple tresses dangled somewhere just below her chin, but not so long that they hid the huge jewels blinging through the hair, or her pretty pointy high cheekbones. Face all made up, with the rouge...glossy pink lipstick...and brows arched like arrows had her looking every bit like she belonged on the cover of any glamour magazine. This was no regular 70-year-old woman with five children, 10 grand, two great-grand, married and divorced a half dozen times. This was a busy executive who made major decisions on the school board, and had been doing so for over forty years, still dating men three decades her junior and living in a home paid off by the money her first ex almost made off with.

But no glamour magazine was out and about on this early evening fall visit to Shugga's house. It was Mrs. Dubois, the nosey next-door neighbor peeking out curtains when Vera pulled up to the curb and hopped out her jazzy Benz. Stepping in a bad pair of goatskin stilettos, tearing up the pavement like she owned it, Mrs. Dubois watched Vera march straight up to Shugga's door.

"Shugga," Vera called out in her perky pretty pink voice, sounding like a suburban cheerleader as she banged on the door. "You in there Shugga? Are you okay?" she called out in the ringing, singing chortling voice. There was a doorbell, but she didn't bother. None of the girls used doorbells. Usually, especially if it was during the day, they walked right in. If the door happened to be locked, then they would knock, usually with their fist. But Vera used the palm of her hand. The reason. It was the nails. She always kept them done, and of course didn't want to afford breaking one.

Mrs. Dubois though, at eighty-something years old, didn't move fast. The best she managed to do by way of hurrying, was tip-toe on two withering legs as fast as she could outside. In her small kitten voice she managed to say, "honey, I'm afraid nobody's in there."

Vera turned around, pulling down the Wang shades to see who was speaking. She just heard the 'I'm afraid' part, and only saw an old fragile white woman hanging onto the step-rail, at four-something in the afternoon wearing a nightgown and nightcap.

"Oh sugar, you don't have to be afraid." And she hurried down the few steps she strutted up, as fast as she could in the stilettos.

"Sweetie, did I wake you," Vera purred on, making her way up the few steps to comfort the old woman. This was where she differed from the girls. She was more of the outward nurturing type. Or rather, more of the mushy nurturing type. In other words, she didn't fall in line with the chit-chat swirling around about Shugga's alleged bigoted neighbors. Even though she came up in the same era as the other girls, seeing some of the same hateful stuff white people did to people of color, she didn't react to this hostile treatment the same. Working in education for so long, and with the top brass more importantly, gave her better insight.

The old woman looked at Vera, her glare a mix of raised alarm and immodest curiosity, and hanging onto the railing for dear life replied, "honey, you probably woke the dead."

"Oh sugar, you don't have to worry about dying," Vera teased. "I bet you're going to outlive me," she winked, though hardly charming the old woman who tried to take a step back as she grabbed both sides of her housecoat with two blue veiny quivering hands.

"Let me help you inside," Vera said, interrupted by the old woman who barked, "No!"

Well, Mrs. Dubois sort of like barked. To Vera's ears what she heard sounded more like a strangled cough. "Sugar, you shouldn't be out here dressed like that," she cooed. "You could catch the pneumonia, honey."

"No!" The old woman shouted again, her voice sounding like the cry of a dying croaking frog. "Leave me alone. Go home! My son-in-law is chief of police!"

That Vera heard. Instantly she threw up both hands, her nails and all the jewels hula-hooping around her wrists and fingers looking more like weapons from Mrs. Dubois's vantage point. "Sugar, I'm not trying to frighten you. We're looking for our friend. Have you seen Shugga?"

"Who!?" rattled the old woman, her eyes opened so wide that it was all that was openly visible.

Vera smiled. Of course. Shugga was Georgia Turner's nickname. She'd been given that name by her father, on the day she was born.

"Georgia," Vera sang. "Have you seen Miss Georgia?"

Clutching her robe so tightly she looked like she had herself in a chokehold, Mrs. Dubois calmed some and replied, "she took off...with a whole lot of bags...weeks ago. Nobody has seen her since."

4.

The funny thing was, a whole week or more had passed before Shugga's name resurfaced. Vera had skipped off to visit another one of the girls who used to live on Gorgas Lane, but had long since relocated to a lush area in an Arizona desert. Mother had moved on too, sweeping herself up in someone else's business with brighter headlights. And Mug, who hadn't yet hitched a ride to swing by Shugga's jobsite, was waiting on the 23 trolley when she bumped into Joyce Jackson.

Digging in her purse, feeling around for her phone that started vibrating, she glanced up, checking for both the trolley and keeping an eye on her surroundings, when Joyce caught her attention. Both spotted each other at the same time.

"Didn't you have a child who went to Anna B. Day," Joyce asked, smiling just enough to show a few tanned teeth.

"Yes, I did," Mug replied. Actually she had six children who went to Anna B. Day, the operative word being 'went'. A half century passed since her children had been in elementary school.

"Leslie, right?"

"Yes, I have a daughter named Leslie," Mug replied. It dawned on her, before it dawned on Joyce, whose chin was tucked in the natty wool green coat, leaving only her popped out searching eyes and dark weathered hands exposed. It was one of the parents whose child was best friends with her daughter. But the two mothers had never really communicated. Back in those days Joyce lived across the tracks, a euphemism people used to express when someone lived on the lower end of a poverty line. And not that Mug and the girls were those kinds of snobs. They just never left the house with their hair in serious disarray, as how Joyce's hair appeared on this chilly, but unbreezy day.

"How is she?" Joyce asked. "You have any grand yet?"

Mug almost cut the woman the stink eye. Unless Joyce had been living beneath rocks, which by the looks of her she very well could have been, there was no way anyone would ask a woman standing on a corner catching a trolley, who had as many children as she had, such a simple-behind question. Of course she had grandchildren, the reason she was standing out in the cold while one of the grands was on the phone asking if she made something to eat.

Mug threw up the 'excuse me one-minute' finger and answered the grand. The conversation didn't last long though. She kept her cabinets full. Her grand knew this, like they knew the routine. The child saw the peanut butter crackers and knew she'd be home in a minute to make dinner. She powered off her phone in no time.

"So, how have you been," she asked Joyce in a similar tone as she replied to the grand.

"Lord, I'm still in shock over Henry's death," Joyce said.

Mug frowned. Henry? Who in the hell was Henry?

"You didn't see it in the paper!?" Joyce nearly shrieked, as if Henry was somebody, sight unseen, everybody knew.

"No, I don't usually read the obituaries," she replied.

Joyce reared back, giving Mug the 'I need to snatch your black card' look. "Henry!" she repeated, that time with her voice elevated. "One of the deacons at ENON! Chile, I think it was an inside job. I bet it was his wife."

So, forget the fact that Mug hadn't read the article and didn't know Henry from Goliath, she really didn't even know Joyce, who was standing there talking to her as if they had been best friends a million years. "I bet it was the wife," Mug went on and obliged the woman. Might as well. She could see the 23 trolley headed their way. This conversation was going to be over in a minute or two.

Joyce reared her head back again, though not with the snatching her black card look. "You know them?"

Mug almost asked who, but caught on rather quickly. "No, I don't know them, but if you say a wife was involved, then it can't be nobody else."

"Ump," Joyce thought out loud. She hadn't thought about it like that. "Well, they found him sitting on the porch... mouth wide open, head reared back and eyes closed. The wife said she thought he was sleep til she figured out he was dead."

"A damn sinning in a shame," Mug replied, faking her disgust. "She oughta' be ashamed of herself. They need to tie her to a tree and beat her with a dustpan!"

Again Joyce jutted her head backwards. A hundred years ago they stopped tying people to trees and whipping them. She started to respond but the trolley pulled up. One after the other, Joyce behind Mug, both hobbled onto the trolley. Hours ago schools closed, so the car wasn't terribly packed. Between the children who left school late and workers who left work early, there still was two 'side-by-side' seats available.

Of course Joyce scooted into the seat right beside Mug, as if they were traveling together. "I'll tell you though," Joyce continued, huffing as she plopped down in the seat, smelling a little like fried chicken. "If I go, I want to go like Henry."

Mug whipped her head around. "If!" she cackled. "Chile, I know you thanked the Lord for letting you get up today, but one day you won't be thanking Him so much!"

"I know that's right," Joyce hummed, obviously missing Mug's point. "I just pray on a peaceful journey."

"Well, I want to go out like Dessa," Mug replied, tickled pink inside. "Do you know her? Odessa Turner?"

Joyce frowned.

"Poor lady," Mug carried on. "Dessa worked herself to the bone. But humble as humble could be. Except for work, she never left the house...all except for this one night. It was her birthday. Her 60th birthday. The people at her job took her to Dave and Busters where she danced until her heart gave out. Died right there on the dance floor... just the way I want to go!"

This seemed to do the trick. It shut Joyce up, until a minute later, about two stops before Mug's stop, Joyce was back at it again.

"You know, I think I remember the Turners. Didn't one of them have a bright-eyed girl who went to Anna B. Day too?"

Sure did. That was Shirley's child Stephy. Shugga never had any kids.

"Oh, but Shugga and Shirley aren't related to Dess—"

"—Yeah, Shirley!" Joyce exclaimed, her eyes turning a few layers less cloudy. "I remember that lady," she recalled. "Real nice lady, always bringing treats to the school."

Joyce continued on, remembering when Shirley drove the little green Volkswagen, way back in the late 60's, before her thoughts sunk recalling Shugga.

"The sister was kind of rough," she cautiously noted. "She was nobody to play with, that's for sure..." and her voice dragged before she abruptly switched memories. "You know, I saw the sister the other day. At Henry's funeral!"

Mug was calling Mother as Mrs. Dubois was telling her grand-daughter about her run-in with Vera. Old as Methuselah the woman had a fragile memory but was a dynamite storyteller.

"That woman run up here with these cat-claws out, coming for me like...hsst...hssst," she described, turning her blue veiny hands into what she thought resembled a cat scratching at someone. "It was terrifying," she explained naturally shaky, as her granddaughter Anabelle kept busy tidying up the woman's monthly bills.

"Oh Nana," Anabelle sighed after a while, for the most part ignoring the old woman as she shoved papers into a drawer. "You know those people don't have the kind of manners we're used to," she replied, before spinning on her heels and asking if the nurse had been by that day.

"The only one who been by here is that cat woman," Mrs. Dubois hissed. "She tried to get in here but I stopped her!"

Now Mrs. Dubois's encounter with Vera happened over a week ago. Anabelle had been to the house a dozen times since then. "Are you sure it wasn't one of the nurses who—"

"—No!" Mrs. Dubois adamantly insisted. "She had no such identification on her. But when I told her my son-in-law was the police chief, you oughta' seen her go then," she boasted chuckling. "She scatted back down them steps real quick. She almost knocked me over she moved so fast!"

"But Nana, what were you doing out of the house? You know better than to open the door to strangers," Anabelle said.

Mrs. Dubois's head bobbed as she thought about what her granddaughter said. "Well, I just come out the house because I saw that woman jiggling Miss Turner's doorknob," she explained. "She was screaming like a crazy woman over there. Obviously, she was trying to break in the place. Probably a crackhead."

Anabelle shook her head. Though she didn't doubt someone had come by, she doubted her grandmother's version of the story. She pulled out her cellphone and called the lady who lived next door on the other side.

"I apologize if I'm disturbing you, but wanted to know if by chance you saw someone over here today," she asked.

Betty hadn't seen a thing that day, but did recall hearing a woman banging and yelling at Miss Turner's house. She didn't think much of it because she had seen the car before, a white Mercedes Benz, and thought she remembered seeing the well-dressed woman before too.

The problem was, the crime rate in the community was so low it was next to nonexistent. The biggest issue was door-to-door solicitors, which she presumed Vera was. Guests ignored the posted signs at the entrance of the semi gated community, as if private property and solicitation strictly prohibited meant all but people on official sales business. It was an aggravation neighbors from time to time had to put up with. Calling police only helped so much, before being ignored like the boy who cried wolf.

"You might want to talk to the woman across the street, Iola," Betty advised. "She has a better view."

Anabelle did just that. She walked across the street and spoke to Iola. "I saw the whole thing," little hunched over Iola explained. "That woman was banging on that door something crazy. I stayed right in my window and watched the whole thing. I was so scared for Lucy."

"I told my grandmother she shouldn't be answering the door," Anabelle sighed, though none of this being what she expected to hear. "Ever since that woman moved over there, I have never been really comfortable," she added.

Iola agreed, her head involuntarily bobbing. "Lucy oughta' know better than coming out the house like that," she sighed. But don't worry doll," she said perking up. "We keep our eyes open around here. I had my phone right in my hand the whole time. I didn't put it down until the woman drove off. Haven't seen her since."

Anabelle started to turn and leave, but like Columbo had one more question. "About what time did this happen," she asked.

"Oh...that happened a few weeks ago...maybe about a month ago..."

6.

"Chile, I met a woman on the trolley today, who said she saw Shugga at some deacon's funeral."

"At some deacon's funeral?" Mother echoed, her face scrunched up. What was Shugga doing at a funeral but can't answer her phone?

"Yeah. You know Henry?

"Henry," Mother again echoed.

Laughing, Mug explained. "Yeah Chile. I ran into one of the kids' classmate's mother," she started. "You remember that woman who used to pull up to the school laying on the horn… who had a mess of kids," she laughed.

Mother squinted trying to remember. "Oh, you're talking about that woman who lived over there by that corner deli them Italians owned, with all them orphans in that nasty house."

"Yeah, that's the one," Mug nodded. "She had about 15 kids, and each one was in one of the kid's classes… from kindergarten all the way up to high-school. Three were in the same grade, and none twins. One of 'em was about old as me and still in 9th grade," she chuckled.

"I just remember that old raggedy house," Mother huffed. "…And all them darn kids! One time I had to drop one of her daughter's off after she spent the night with Terri. Chile, I never found the front door. All I remember was a snaggle-tooth woman hanging out an upstairs window with hair standing over her head and a comb stuck in it."

"Yeah, that's who I saw today," Mug laughed. "Only she had taken the comb out."

"Well, thank God," Mother scoffed rolling her eyes.

"Yeah, but it didn't look like anything, comb or otherwise, had touched that head. She could've at least put a hat on. I had to sit next to her for ten blocks smelling fried chicken the whole way."

"Chile, I don't know how you do it," Mother chuckled. "You'll never catch me on the bus!"

"Yeah well, the woman said she saw Shugga at Henry's funeral!"

"Henry," Mother asked again. "Who the hell is Henry?"

"Girl, one of ENON's deacons! Didn't you read it in the paper," she laughed.

"Girl stop," Mother scoffed, playfully rolling her eyes. "You know ENON got a zillion-deacons. That could be anybody! Have you talked to Shugga yet?"

"Chile no," Mug huffed. "You know how Deb is... with her sometimey self," she fussed. "Her and I got into it the other day. She had the nerve to tell me it wasn't her fault I brought her here!"

"Girl, did you take her back?"

"Lord," Mug dragged out, eyes closed and rocking. "You know I wanted to," she said shaking her head too. "Chile, had it been a few years back, she wouldn't be here."

This was how Mug acquired her nickname, rather late in life albeit, considering how most got nicknamed as children. Her husband gave her the name, in lieu of calling her pug. To him, and no one argued, she resembled a bull dog. She was a stout little chocolate woman who, until people got to know her, always seemed to be frowning. The only difference between her and the bull dog, other than the obvious of course, was the hair. She wore hers short, in a curly gold afro. And she kept it tight too. The edges and cue'd sides, without chemicals, except for the color, made her whole look easy on the eyes.

But as it used to be said, she was a rough customer. She loved to laugh and had a heart of gold, and yet it was open knowledge, Mug was no one to fool around with.

7

So, imagine the following day, Mug hustling up the street after climbing off the 23 trolley, bone tired having spent a six-hour work day directing thousands of calls and hundreds of visitors, to spot off in the distance police activity swarmed SWAT style around her house. The closer she got, the more her waddling hoofy walk, turned into all hoof. Trouble had definitely landed on the Davies front doorstep.

She had to call on the Lord. "Lord, help me control what I can control, and please take the wheel for everything outside my watch," she prayed.

Two detectives stood on her front porch. One about 6-foot. The other, 5-feet...wide. She walked right on by as if it wasn't her house. That's what the Lord instructed her to do. She was explicitly told she wouldn't make it up the front steps. And even if she did, there was no telling what she might do or say if one of the officers got out of line, which she had no doubt was going to happen. She was too old, and for darn sure too tired, to be trying to pull both feet out of her mouth. She could wind up a convalescent, the one small chuckle she got out of the hoof, imagining her butterball behind rolling around to get around.

Like an escaped convict on the run, she hoofed it an extra block to reach the back of the house, which due to her short stature made the journey through the alleyway double the hoof. Twice one of her knees almost caught her forehead.

Huffing and puffing she entered the house through the back door. Got inside and the first thing she saw was Oscar, sitting at the dining room table, slumped in the chair with the TV off and his back facing the front door.

"What the devil you doing sittin' in here like this," she fussed. "You hear them cops out there knocking on the door!?"

"Aww, let 'em knock," he grumbled. "They don't do nothing but run around lookin' for niggas to lock up."

"Just as stubborn as an old bull," Mug fumed, slamming her purse on the table. The man had grown more ornery each year they stayed married, and so far they had been married 49 years.

"I'ma let 'em in here, so you better run on upstairs and grab a coat or pillow or something," she wryly chuckled.

Oscar ignored her. Truthfully, Mug should've been concerned, but she was just too darn tired. At this point she didn't care who the law was after. Him, her, or one of the kids or grandkids. They could've brought one of those old blue and white paddy wagons as far as she was concerned, and locked up the entire block.

And yet, also true, she knew that much police activity hadn't come for her. By Oscar's demeanor, who in 49-years she still hadn't figured out, she assumed it wasn't him either. The most he ever did was cry a bucket of tears telling everyone how he couldn't survive a day without her, but the minute they got home and he put down the drink and she picked up a drink, her choice Vodka, his Scotch, he went right back to acting like he hated the day they met. Therefore, it had to be something one of the kids had done.

She stormed to the front door and turned each tumbler like she was twisting his ear, or lips. She just might've killed him that night had she slugged up those steps and found the door bolted down like he had it. "God help you if they don't carry you out of here," she shouted back at him. She swung the door open to greet two shiny badges thrust in her face. "Ma'am, are you Julia Davis?"

"Davies," she angrily corrected. It had been years since she had any personal dealings with the police. The very last time was when she was at a Mall and an old white woman accused her of assault. Police had her in cuffs before noticing her grandbaby's bloodied face. The old white woman had done that with her purse. Slapped her grandchild dead in the face, mad because the child was in her way. Just nasty. Nothing but pure hate, which back then Mug met hate with more hate. The old woman was lucky though, and perhaps Mug was too. She only got to hit the old bat once, on account of some shoppers going the extra mile pinning her down. But then she almost landed in cuffs a second time, after the cuffs were removed and her stumpy self left the floor demanding the old woman be put in cuffs the same way.

Damn giving that mean old woman medical attention. She wanted the old battlelax thrown to the ground, and a knee put in her back and handcuffed too. That was the last time she had any major run-ins with police, back in her heyday when she was whipping lots of butts and taking no names. But that was over a decade ago. The grandchild she had out that day was now 17-years old.

"Are you sure," asked the taller detective, quickly switching his line of examination when Mug gave him the look. "We stopped by earlier but the gentleman who answered the door said no Julia Davis lived here."

Mug didn't bother to correct him that time. Using her head to gesture at Oscar, who still sat with his back facing the front door, she asked, "would that man sitting over there facing a blank TV be who you talked to earlier?"

A part of her wanted to step aside and bait the police to draw their service revolvers and go ballistic unloading on her mullish husband.

"That's him," chuckled the round detective, his belly jumping like a bowl of jelly.

"Please don't aim too high," Mug wryly replied, mostly addressing the round man who looked like he enjoyed good entertainment. "He doesn't have much up there. He's suffering from Alzheimer's and dementia."

"I don't have no Alt's-heimers," Oscar shouted from the dining room, turning 90 degrees in the chair bracing for a fight. "That's a bunch of bullshit," he fumed, rising from the chair like he was going to do something.

"Mannnn...you better have a seat," Mug warned. "Don't make me get that shoebox out of your closet. I'll turn you in for sure."

Both detective's eyes flickered like the bulb of a camera flashing. Mug was speaking probable cause and search warrant language.

"Don't pay him no mind," Mug whispered with a wink. "He's harmless..."

"Ugh...yeah...okay..." stuttered the taller detective. "We only came here to speak with you about Georgia Turner."

Nobody knew it, and that being none of the girls knew it was Chief Steele, the son-in-law of Mrs. Dubois who sent detectives to pay Mug a visit.

Blame him. Blame the man who had a job to do, and a very important job at that. He didn't have time nor resources to order a baby-sitting service to watch a neighborhood where nothing ever happened anyway, especially given it was general knowledge Georgia Turner, on her own volition, was seen putting six large suitcases in the trunk of her car and taking off.

The quickest solution, and brilliant on top of efficient, was doing exactly what he did, having one stringent message delivered officially. Go bang on a door in Africa, because it was exactly where the girl's Shugga went. All he wanted was his wife's grandmother and the other neighbors left alone in their historically peaceful and quiet semi-gated decent community.

Mug picked up the phone and called Mother right away. "Chile, guess where Shugga at?"

"Where?"

"Chile, Shugga is in the Motherland," Mug chuckled. "She done went on vacation!"

"Ump," Mother huffed, not particularly happy to hear this news. Mug knew it. It always ticked Mother off when she heard someone had taken vacation, especially when they had escaped to a far-off exotic place while she was at home. The girls got a kick out of torturing her, flaunting stories about other people's trips and watching her tear up every time she saw a plane in the sky and wasn't on it.

"Detectives came by here today and told me," Mug rubbed in.

"Detectives?" Mother replied with a raised brow.

"Girl, I came up the street to find the house surrounded by police and two detectives on my doorstep," Mug laughed. "I thought the law had finally caught up to Oscar, with all them porn videos he be in here watching day and night...thinking I don't know," she said switching tones to scoff. "I hoped they had come here to take his ba'hind away, and lock him up for good."

Mug didn't really mean that, but it sure perked up Mother's mood. Few things were better than sharing misery with a good friend. "Well, when they come for Oscar, please have them swing by here and take Joe too!"

"Oh, so Joe watches that nasty mess too?"

"Chile, he got more porn in his drawers than socks and underwear," Mother replied. "I told him, he better not get a hold of any of that underage stuff. They'll drag him on out of here and he'll never see the light of day!"

"It's the same thing I told Oscar," Mug fussed. "Thing about it is, his dumb ba'hind don't know what the ages of them girls are. I don't know why they watch that stuff anyway," she huffed. "Ain't like they can do anything with it."

"Ain't that the truth," Mother agreed. "Joe's stuff so shribbled up he look like a woman. If it wasn't for that big 'ole sac hanging down to his knees I'd swear he was one!"

"Chile, where did it go?!"

"Oh, Joe never was much in bed," Mother inserted. "To this day I don't know how we ended up with any kids."

"Well Oscar used to have it. He used to want it morning, noon and night," Mug recalled. "Sometimes he got on my nerves so bad, jumping up and down on me like a bunny rabbit. Serves him right. Now he miserable, having used up all his fuck strokes," she laughed loud.

Mother kept quiet for a minute. Years ago, when they were in their early 20's, she had the biggest crush on Oscar. He used to dress so cool, with the tams cocked to the side and silk shirts he kept open showing pebbles of hair and beautiful jewelry he wore around his neck. He had the best sense of humor too, and the prettiest smile. Big, beautiful white teeth, and he could dance his behind off. The two of them, Mother and Oscar, used to wipe up a dance floor. They kept everyone entertained, mesmerized by their cha-cha. Mug seemed like she hated him though. Mother used to catch her sitting at the bar, glaring darts at him. When Oscar wasn't stealing the attention in the middle of the room dancing his butt off, he'd be stealing the show getting his behind whipped. Him and Mug used to fight like cats and dogs, even though everyone knew he loved her to death.

"Yeah, Joe could be in here fixing up our cabinets, or out there working on the yard," Mother said, her voice thinned out, saddened a little by the good old days long gone. "You oughta' see our yard," she got back to scoffing. "Look like a bed for rattlesnakes!"

"Oh my goodness, you should see what Oscar did to my dishwasher," Mug joined in. "Girl, him and his brother got to fooling underneath my sink, hooking up a hose I thought they borrowed from the fire department!"

Mother fell back laughing. "But now, why were that many police over at your house telling you about Shugga?

A few days later Mother was downtown in Panache having her hair done when she bumped into another one of the girls from Gorgas Lane. Myrtle.

"Woman! What have you been up to? I haven't seen you in ages," Myrtle howled in her native busty voice. "I used to see Joe sittin' on the porch... sleepin'," she chuckled, coughing and trying to clear her throat, due to years of smoking. "...Now I drive by and it looks like ghosts live there."

Mother smiled. Even though Myrtle lived a couple of blocks away, unlike Mug they weren't as close. Their social class sort of diverged. Myrtle hob-knobbed with the Joneses, preferring to rub shoulders and elbows with the upper-class, those who earned over 100K and held important jobs...such as Vera. Mother never made that much money, not even when she managed a department at an insurance firm making almost 50K a year. What sealed the friendship was their children, and the fact they both lived on Gorgas Lane for over half a century.

Their girls had been friends since kindergarten, and gone to high-school and college together. They pledged the same sorority, were each other's maid and matron of honor, godparents to each other's children, and worked in the same government office. Their girls were inseparable, calling each other sisters, which naturally created a bond, just not as tight as the bond Mother shared with Mug, and Shirley.

"And what's that on your finger," Myrtle blurted, eyeballing a large rock on Mother's ring finger, clearly a zirconia. "What? Joe bought you another diamond," she chuckled.

Mother smiled again. Besides her busty throaty voice and hob-knobbing, albeit of a pleasant gregarious nature, Myrtle also was loud. VERY LOUD. The woman couldn't whisper to save her life. She sat right beside Mother, waiting on her stylist like three or four other women waiting, and everyone in the lounge, from the front of the salon to the washing bowls, was a part of this exchange.

"Chile," Mother finally got out, "I've been working. Everybody don't have it like you, who got to fully retire at 62. I'm still robbing Peter to pay Paul!"

Many in the salon laughed, sort of siding with Mother.

Myrtle only chuckled, her throaty laugh sounding like she was gurgling gravel. Few things really offended her. "I still work," she replied anyway, coughing and patting her chest. "I work for Tony, helping to manage his campaign. We've got to get the idiot out of office," she chuckled, along with a number of others nodding their head in full agreement, knowing just what local politician she was talking about.

"So, when's the last time you've seen Vera," Mother went on and asked.

"I haven't seen Vera since she left for Arizona," Myrtle replied. "You know Elaine has a mansion out there. Vera sent pictures. Lawd, I thought she was at Hugh Heffner's!" and she laughed long and hard on that one. She must have coughed for five minutes. Ladies in the salon had scrolled through all the photos on her phone before she caught her breath.

"Ooo! That is my dream home," one remarked.

"Look at that pool," another commented.

"White marble floors," another marveled.

Mother only huffed, her emotions kind of hung on a hook. She didn't need to see more than one photo before she had to look away. It looked like everyone was having fun, and she wasn't there.

"Well, I hope she enjoys herself," Mother scoffed out the corner of her mouth, speaking of Vera. "When she gets back here, she might be interested in knowing there is a warrant for her arrest."

"WARRANT," Myrtle screeched, causing all heads to swing their way. "Why would there be a warrant out for Vera's arrest!?"

Myrtle called Vera ASAP, like before she left the salon, while both she and Mother were under hair-dryers. There was no telling what might happen once she left the salon. At 72-years old she couldn't trust her memory.

"Chile, did you know a warrant is out for your arrest," she belted into the phone. No greeting whatsoever. Not that there needed to be one.

Vera's eyes popped open, though like a rose opening in fast motion. "A warrant out for my arrest," she choraled, her lips parted, but more so mimicking a smile. "Who in the world would put an APB out on me," she sang, now clearly grinning.

"The police, that's who," Myrtle belted.

"But why," Vera sang.

"Mother said Shugga's neighbors called the cops on you for disturbing the peace."

Vera looked up and thought back. Last time she had been over to Shugga's house was weeks ago, and all she did was knock on Shugga's door, but got no answer. "You think I should call the police and turn myself in?"

"I'd call a lawyer before I did that," Myrtle advised. "You know police can't get a story straight to save their life."

"Maybe I should call Mother," Vera said thinking out loud. "I need to figure out why the police would tell her something like that instead of coming to me. Everybody know where I stay..."

And that sure was the truth. Vera got around, and in more ways than a few. She had been married four times...

that everyone knew of... and she was still divorced...and still dating. But it wasn't only men parading in and out of her home. Aside from a few women who traipsed uninvited over to her home, off-the-handle mad about one of the men she had been seeing in strict disobedience of what was written in the Bible, she knew every single dignitary in the city.

Politicians, police, clergy, the heads at the Board of Education...everybody who was somebody she knew.

"Well, Mother is right here with me," Myrtle said. "We're in Panache getting our hair done."

"Well, let me speak to Mother. I need to find out what's going on here..."

"Here," Myrtle said, handing Mother her phone.

But Mother was beneath the dryer, with her eyes closed. Loud as Myrtle talked, she hadn't heard a word. She had to lift the dryer, looking at Myrtle asking with her eyes for an explanation as to who was on the other line and why she needed to speak with them.

"Hello," Mother said, apprehensive about whose voice she was going to hear.

"Mother, what's going on!? This is Vera. Myrtle said the police is after me."

Vera didn't need to introduce herself. Everyone and their mother knew that singing voice. She didn't say words, she sang them... like Patti LaBelle, Aretha, or anyone with a distinct sound. And one of them peachy clean, Southern pitches, much over-done. For those who didn't know any better, she sounded Southern bell phony.

"Chile," Mother laughed. "Is this the only way I can get a call back from you? You were supposed to let us know what was up with Shugga."

"Oh Chile, I must have gotten caught up," Vera lazily replied. "I'm coming and going so much I can't even keep up with myself."

"I know what you mean," Mother agreed. "Yesterday I was looking all over the house for my glasses and all be dern, mad as a hornet and hours later found them right on my face."

Vera squealed. "That happened to me! Now I always check my face first," she laughed.

"So, I hear you've been lounging poolside in Hugh's mansion," Mother cut in, interrupting the laughter.

"Huh?" Vera didn't catch Mother's drift.

"Elaine," Mother explained. "I hear you visited Elaine's mansion."

"Oh my Lord, yes," Vera choraled. "Chile, her place is fabulous! Just gorgeous! And we had a blast," she replied, feet kicked up, lounging on a white chaise, albeit in her home. "I told her it would be the perfect place for all of us girls to unite and sort of celebrate a long-needed reunion!"

Bingo! Mother's ears popped open. "I'm on my way! Getting my airline ticket now. Send me the address and date when you get it," she joked.

Vera loved it. She loved Mother's vibe and eagerness to blindly get up and go. "Yazzzzz," she sang. "Don't you worry Mother. Soon as we have a date, you will be the first I call..." she schmoozed, breaking the jamboree to ask... "...but what's this I hear about police out to get me?"

"Oh girl, you have to talk to Mug," Mother replied, dismissing the question by a wave of the hand. "She was the one who talked to the police."

Vera's chat with Mug went a lot quicker and with far fewer frills. It wasn't that there was any discord between the two women, but more due to the fissure in personalities. Mug didn't care for Vera's fru-fru banter.

"Mug darling, what in the world were the po-po doing asking you questions about me," Vera wanted to know.

See, this was the kind of banter Mug snarled at. The only one that called her darling, or should have been calling her darling, was Oscar. And po-po? She couldn't stand Vera talking down to her like that. Just because she worked at the board of education and not in a crummy social services building didn't mean she was a dumb-dumb. But be it as it was, she couldn't argue that Vera wasn't the sweetest woman on the face of earth.

"Chile, they sent SWAT over here about your going over to Shugga's and raising hell. They said you were out there acting a plum fool."

"Oh Lord," Vera gasped. "All I did was knock on the door."

"Well, it must have been some hellified knocking. The police said you woke the whole neighborhood."

"Ump," Vera chuckled thinking back. "That ole' woman did say I had raised the dead," she squealed laughing.

"And that you did doll baby," Mug chuckled too, though more so for the nick she managed to throw in.

"Still, I don't see why they want to arrest me for that."

"Arrest you? Nobody said nothing about arresting you."

"Well not according to Mother and Myrtle..."

"Myrtle!?" Mug shrieked. She hadn't talked to Myrtle in ages, and they lived no more than a block apart. What did she know about what police said to her?

"What's Myrtle up to nowadays anyway?" Mug asked. "Last I heard she was at the Maryland House waitin' for a tow!"

"Ieeeek," Vera squealed. She heard about that story too…Myrtle calling herself driving to visit her daughter who lived in Virginia, and getting scared on 95. Her daughter and son-in-law had to go get her, and after the visit had to drive her home. Myrtle hadn't been on 95 since. And that happened a summer ago.

"Chile, Mertie is doing just fine. You know she—"

"—Oh sweetie, I got someone on the other line," Mug cut in. "Let me call you back. You're still at the same number, right?"

"Well, you can get me on my—"

"—Oh sugar pie, my pencil done ran out of ink," Mug said cutting her off again, juggling the TV remote and phone, her version of multitasking.

"Hang on…Ooo!…better yet," and she dropped the phone trying to increase the volume on the remote. But when she accidently changed the channel, she picked up the phone.

"Girl, you know where I stay," she said after eventually getting back to the channel she was watching.

Confused, trying to figure out what was going on in Mug's house, Vera kept silent, waiting for a clue. She knew Mug was up to something, but didn't know she was trying to find out if the dumb ba'hind woman from Kentucky, who betted all her money on Jeopardy, and got the answer wrong, was going to lose against the guy from Philly who had a whole whopping ten dollars left!

"Oh, dammit!" Mug huffed. She missed it! She missed hearing what everybody had to say.

Except for the background noise going on as she talked with Mug, Vera hardly noticed much else, and didn't mind being hung up on at all. She was a busy woman too. Over the years she cut oodles and oodles of people short when she was tight on time. But her freedom was important, which included her peace of mind.

"Barry, some friends called me the other day and told me police had a warrant out for my arrest. Is that something I should be worried about?"

Barry was an executive at the Board of Education. The President of Programs. He dealt a lot with policy. Plus he was married to a fine lawyer. That being fine in her reputation with winning corporate corruption cases, for defendants. Usually, anyone pulled on the carpet for white collar crimes had already been blacklisted and pretty much written off; signed, sealed and airlifted over to permanent destitution. Rarely did people return from those scandals, all but for the clients Rozzell handled.

With a raised brow Barry asked what was the crime.

"I'm not sure," Vera replied. "An old friend had asked me to check on another friend, which I ran by there, knocked on the door, and now... and I'm speaking weeks later, I hear police are after me about the incident. They said something about I was disturbing the peace."

"I wouldn't worry about it," Barry shrugged, slipping into his suit jacket. "But to be on the safe side I'll call a few people and check it out."

Carmela Moore and Julianna Price, junior journalists for the pilot reality television program 'WomenStandUp', were having dinner in a swanky restaurant not far from the parkway. Prime real estate described here. These two young ladies were amateurs, but not low class by any means. They were aggressive, smart women taught the world was their oyster. All they had to do was want it, and go after it. Boss women many called them, though in the middle of an oyster war they weren't yet ready to sell the image.

Carmela, as it happened to be, were one of the ladies waiting for a stylist on the day Myrtle got to belting the girls' business all over the salon, sharing photos and telling stories, oblivious to who all was listening.

"I think I have a story Marsha will love," Carmela leaned over and whispered to Julianna. There was no paisley reason for leaning over the way she did. They were dining in shark infested waters. Unlike Myrtle, on that blasé day in the salon, she was fully aware of the pandemic of hungry journalists sitting all around them. One was apt to lift the story she worked up in her mind.

"Really," Julianna cooed, desperate as any young journalist clawing their way to the top of the credits' list. But in the past few weeks she had given her career serious reexamination, thinking perhaps she had set her sights in the wrong direction. Instead of reaching for credit, she could elbow her way into schools to teach youngins, a lot younger than her, how to properly go about getting scoops, and thus credit.

Going viral was going overrated. For months Marsha had been shooting down their leads, claiming their stories were putty, or a snoozer, or mooner, or a slum dunk magnet, meaning the story might go viral alright, but at the expense of 'Women-StandUp.'

"Yah, I was in Panache a few days ago and overheard these women talking," Carmela started to explain. "So, you know these aren't the average street type women—"

"—Wait, how do you know that?"

"Ummm, like hello," Carmela said, using her hands and eyes to draw out the whole duh look. "Panache! Like who gets their hair done in Panache but women who own their own homes, thus have careers," she went on gesturing, using her eyes and hands to dramatize the wealth she was speaking of. "I mean, iPhones...Coach handbags...driving Cadillacs..." she rattled off, also using her fingers to count these laurels. "Like, hello," she said again for the knock-knock wake up effect. "I'm talking women who have money and reputations to protect!"

Julianna got it, but hadn't caught on to how this would help women, or more importantly, them. "Marsha isn't looking to be bumped off her perch you know. She hates women who have it all pulled together."

"That's not true," Carmela replied. Journalism, indeed was tricky, as Julianna implied. They couldn't go too far left, or right. The winning story had to be middle of the road balanced. So Carmela leaned over the table and whispered, "one of the friends is missing and someone is covering it up as a vacation."

Julianna stared at Carmella. "Are you sure," she gasped. This was as middle of the road as a story got. There was mystery, whodunit intrigue, and it was a high likelihood a man was the animus. Few stories trumped this type story. It covered all three corners, plus, no one...intentionally, or at least outwardly... was trying to bump anyone off a peddle stool.

"Positive," Carmela giggled. "I heard the entire conversation. I even recorded it."

"Boss," Julianna smiled, taking a deep breath as she fists bumped Carmela, sprinkling the star dust over their half-eaten meal. "But how are we going to use the recording? You know—"

"—We're not," Carmela quickly inserted before correcting herself. "I mean, we're not going to play it for Marsha. We're going to study it to..." and using her fingers for quotes she added "...come up with creative ways to get personal interviews and inside scoops. You know, sort of like poking hot coals."

"Oh my gosh. That's genius," Julianna cheered. "Yah! I love it! Let the dogs take out the trash! We'll be the real heroes!"

"Ummm, that's shero," Carmela said. "And let's settle down," she added. "I don't think there's that much to the story."

Instantly Julianna's face dropped. "But why—"

"—Because that's the whole point," Carmela winked.

It was about 7pm and dark outside when Mother and Joe were carrying groceries from the trunk of her Cadillac up a few steps and into the house. This was about the one and only thing they did as a couple. The one surviving masculine trait Joe maintained.

"Hey Mother," came a voice from inside a metallic blue BMW.

Mother turned around and pried open her eyes. She didn't recognize the vehicle or the two women inside, but lots of people drove by the house shouting out her name. She and Joe had been living in the house since 66'. Forty-seven years, between their children, friends, neighbors, co-workers and relatives they had accumulated a lengthy list of anyone liable to greet them this way, giving Mother no cause to be rude.

"Didn't you have a daughter who went to Girls High," asked the passenger hanging out the window. She was a pretty girl. Long good hair. Light skin. Narrow nose. Big bright eyes and pretty teeth. No one mother instantly recognized, but someone her daughter could've gone to school with. This one just looked like that Girls High type.

"Yes, Mona, she did," Mother replied half smiling. The bag she balanced on one knee got heavy. She had to get up the steps and in the house before that one ceramic knee gave out.

"Why don't you let us help you get those bags in the house," the young woman offered, coached by the driver, though nothing Mother picked up on.

BMW parked the young girls hopped out the car. Mother waited. One girl was taller than the other, though both were pretty slim, and under better lighting, noticeably much too youthful to have gone to school with Mona. They couldn't have been a day over twenty-five.

The passenger introduced herself as Chloe. She graduated in 94', more than a decade after Mona. But Mother didn't question the discrepancy. Maybe she met her daughter at a job fair or something. Once all the bags were in the house, and after a lot of small chatter between trips from the car to the house, Mother introduced the young women to Joe. Hardly enthused he had no interest in either shaking hands, or smiling. In fact, he appeared quite irritated. During one trip into the house, while the girls were outside giggling among themselves, he grunted at Mother, scoffing about her being so naive, allowing strangers in the house.

"You always fussing at me for letting strangers in and talking to them on the phone," he growled. "…But I guess it's okay for you to do it!"

Mother ignored him though. She invited the girls to sit down at their dining room table, offering them Coca-Cola while Joe grunted, slamming cabinets and drawers before schlepping upstairs with a cup of coffee.

"I don't know what's wrong with him," Mother said apologetically. "Usually he's all over young girls pretty as you two. You should see the stack of porn he keeps in his closet."

Chloe's and April's eyes doing doughnuts in opposite directions liked to have given them away. Their jaws dropped to the floor. They declined the invite to sit down, backing their way out the door.

"Well, tell Mona we said hello," Chloe offered, as April chimed in over her shoulder. "And you guys be careful going grocery shopping so late at night," she giggled.

Surprise! Surprise! Thank goodness Shirley called! All week Mother wanted to talk to her but hesitated calling after the small messy situation she sort of like stirred. Wasn't no since starting more mess with Shirley thousands of miles away. She couldn't do a darn thing about her sister's sudden absence.

"Hey girlfriend," Shirley chirped. "What are you doing up this early," she chuckled. Sounded like she was sitting on a balcony, feet up, facing a peachy London sun with one of the grandbabies snuggled comfortably on her bosom. Shugga's whereabouts probably the very last thing on her mind.

"Chile, I can't sleep like I used to," Mother cackled. "Every three or four hours I'm back up and in the fridge."

"That's what they say," Shirley chuckled. "We start out as babies and end up babies."

"Girl, ain't that the truth," Mother agreed. "But at least I won't end up bald head. My mother said I was born with a head full of hair."

"Yeah, but it hardly will matter since you weren't born with teeth and potty trained," she teased.

"Look, hopefully I'll be babbling and out of my mind too, so none of it will matter anyway," Mother teased back.

"Well, I'm out here ready to lose mine," Shirley replied to her girlfriend's surprise. "These are some nasty behind white folk out here. 'Bout as bad as the ones back home."

"Oh no," Mother sighed. "I thought London was the crème de la crème."

"Chile, it's the crim of de' crimes! A dern sinning in a shame the way these people talk to you like you're stupid. And these black ones are simple ba'hinds too," she vented. "But what irks me is this dern husband Stephy married. Thinks he knows every dern thing with a master's degree that's not worth a scoop of poop. Chile, he's out here parking cars!"

Welp, that sounded about right, even if the confession came as a surprise. Mother didn't get to go to the wedding, since it was held on the Irish Sea on a resort island, and since too, the real reason, she wasn't invited, largely due to being in the hospital, recovering from gastro surgery.

Still, from Shirley's own mouth she claimed Stephy had married an aristocrat, a man descendent from a line of nobles. Supposedly the man had a thousand different degrees, spoke a hundred different languages, had traveled the globe, and worked in one of the palaces...with the real royals. Now this? She would have never guessed.

"Seriously," Mother asked shocked, reclining in her chair and crossing her legs, open to hearing more.

"Chile, I done booked my ticket," Shirley huffed. "I'm out of here on the first thing smokin'!"

"But I bet you're going to miss them grandbabies..."

"No, Mr. Smartass is sending them to a nanny," Shirley scoffed. "Apparently holding them is interfering with their cognitive growth. Makes me sick," she snarled.

"Well, at least he has the money to—"

"—And that's just it," Shirley fumed. "He don't have a dime! His father has the money. He's the one paying for everything."

"But—"

—But Shirley cut her off she was so angry. "Chile, that man came over here one day, talking to me like I was dirt," she scoffed. "Had the nerve to tell me how much money he was giving Stephy, like I gave a damn! Hell, that's his son's problem! Shucks, that's his wife! He married her! They're supposed to take care of her and these babies! The Fool!" she fumed.

"Oh good Lord," Mother sighed. She had no idea.

"I'll tell you one thing," Shirley continued. "If Stephy don't wake up and see the writing on the wall, she's going to end up out here with three babies, alone, up the creek."

Whoa! Talk about not knowing the things that really went on inside the Joneses homes. Mother didn't know what to say, so she said nothing, and let the real story roll... which Shirley continued on that roll for several minutes.

"Child blind as a bat," Shirley went on. "These people don't have no more money than I do!"

And that was a mouthful. Rumor was, Shirley received a huge settlement after Chester left. Shugga let this one out of the bag, though Shirley never admitted it nor denied it, unlike how she found spaces to casually slip in mention of Stephy's noble in-laws, and how they sent for her, and paid her rent for two months so that she could be with her daughter on the birth of the triplets.

"Girl can barely get a cleaning job," Shirley fumed. "Shoot! I didn't spend all that money on her education for her to be out here living like this!"

It was a good minute after the several minutes of irate ranting before Shirley took it down a notch, when Mother was finally able to ask if she had talked to Shugga lately.

"You know Shugga's not speaking to me," Shirley snapped. "Last I heard, she's supposed to be living somewhere in Africa...about to marry some African prince!"

Mother couldn't get off the phone fast enough. Her ears were loaded. Like a rowboat in the middle of an ocean, packed with drunks all wanting to dance at the same time. She had to hang up on Shirley. Well, not figuratively. The call ended on a somewhat cordial note. That being they both said good-bye at the same time, though it was a close call. With them whooshing sounds colliding in her head the way they were, Shirley almost got hung up on.

"Mug, girl! Did you know Shugga was in Africa about to get married!?"

"Chile, I ain't fooling around about Shugga no more! Besides, I was the one who told you!"

"Well, I can't imagine Shugga went to Africa to marry an African prince! Did you know the man was rich!?"

"Girl, didn't I say I ain't foolin' around with Shugga!"

But Mother hardly heard Mug with the whooshing in her head. She continued talking, almost rambling. "But Chile, I honestly thought Shugga might be gay—"

"—Gay!?" Mug shrieked. "Chile, you must be out of your mind. Do you see the size of that Bible she totes around?"

The size of the Bible Shugga carried around, indeed was no joke. Relieving her eyes of added pressure, and making sure she didn't miss anything, she got her hands on an oversized King James version, acquired from a museum…in Greece… possibly why she got in so many arguments on scripture, and exactly why Mother would even question her sexuality. Shugga was more than an open book.

"Yeah, I've seen it," Mother argued. "And I've also seen Shugga defending what's in that book!" And not one person had yet to beat her in a word war on scripture either!

"Girl, I don't have time for none of Shugga's nonsense—hang on, somebody is at my door—better yet, let me call you back."

On this day everyone was getting on Mug's nerves. Her kids, the grand, her co-workers, Oscar, Mother...everybody. And then she opened the door to a woman standing on her porch looking like she was about to try and sell her another headache.

"Yeah, can I help you?" Mug snarled.

The young woman smiled, paying the snarl no mind, to lay on Mug how someone at Social Services had nominated her for a Shero award. The accolade recognized role models in the community, in which according to the woman at the door, Mug had been a Shepard. She had been the light at the end of someone's long dark tunnel, going above and beyond helping displaced women and children.

"May we come in," the young woman asked.

Mug looked around, looking for the we part.

"Oh, my associate is in the car," the woman politely smiled, waving at Julianna sitting in the metallic blue BMW. "We want to get an exclusive from you," she continued. "I don't know if you watch 'WomenStandUp', but we are journalists for that show. A lot of our subjects get picked up by Oprah."

Though Mug hadn't heard of either 'WomenStandUp' or the Shero award, she indeed knew Oprah. Not personally, but who didn't know Oprah!?!

Her mood pivoted 360-degrees. Stepping aside she grinned her widest smile, opening her door, heart and grin wide enough for a fleet of egos the size of the Queen Mary towing Taj Mahal to sail through.

"Y'all come on in here and get out this cold," Mug beamed.

She cleared the dining room table, wiping it vigorously and set out placemats she hadn't used in ages. A few minutes later she had whipped up leftovers; Southern fried chicken, ham, collard greens, potato salad, cornbread cut into snack bites for the snooty, and had that on the table too. Going an extra mile she also opened a bag of mints, aimed at keeping the girls serenading her and asking questions for as long as air remained in their lungs.

"So, how long have you worked for social services," Julianna asked, taking careful bites of the cornbread squares, cupping her hand beneath her chin to catch the crumbs.

"Since I was sixteen," Mug replied. "It was my first job. I never left. It's my calling. I've always loved helping people."

No sooner than she left that rosy sentiment one of her grandchildren came in the house. The child had her coat hanging on her head and was wearing flip-flops, without socks.

"Mu, can I have—"

"—Take your ba'hind upstairs and put some socks on," Mug hissed out the corner of her mouth.

"But Mu—"

"—Did you hear what I said," Mug hissed again. "And wipe your nose," she shouted over her shoulder. "I'll deal with you in a minute!"

The child schlepped upstairs, whimpering as she went.

"That's my oldest daughter's child," Mug explained, not missing a beat, despite the skeptical expressions watching her. "Family first," she chirped. "I have three generations in here!"

"Wonderful," Carmela eased out, hardly the expression on her face. "But how do you address the generational curses that continue to plague women?"

"Huh?" Mug thought Carmela switched languages and started speaking Cantonese. "Generational curses?" she echoed.

"Well, yah," Carmela replied. "You know, women getting stuck in traditional gender-based roles, having to do all the domestic stuff pertaining to taking care of children?"

Mug looked from one girl to the other. "Chile please, neither one of y'all would be sittin' here askin' that question if a woman hadn't stepped up to clean ya' ba'hinds and feed you."

"Ugh yeah...we get that," Carmela jumped in. "But how do you feel about men and women sharing chores? You know, so that women can get out of ruts and get better jobs to stand on their own."

"Let me put it like this," Mug replied. "Like I tell women coming through the system crying that mess. Everybody can't be a bandleader. At some point we have to stop playing victim, which really is a sign of weakness, and accept what is."

Julianna and Carmela stared, but didn't speak. Though Mug hardly noticed with her eyes closed and head throwed back the way it was.

"Men can't nurse babies," she continued. "Women are naturally built to handle that, like men are bigger and stronger and sometimes dumber... you know most of 'em only think with one part of their body..." and she paused when Carmela and Julianna laughed. They liked that part.

"We shouldn't turn up our noses at so-called traditional roles," she said, another part where she got the frown. "I know young people don't like hearing that, but it's true. It doesn't mean women can't pick up saws and work like men, but most will never be able to chop down as many trees as men...and to tell the truth, why would we want to?"

"To be independent," Julianna almost argued.

"Let me ask you something," Mug said, popping her lips after licking the back of a spoon. "How long have you girls been living in the city?"

"We grew up in Exton," Julianna started. "But—"

"—Un huh, like I thought," Mug interrupted. "But tell me something. Would you beg God to make children be born deaf, blind, deformed and retarded?"

Carmela and Julianna's eyes liked to have popped out its sockets, the look they gave Mother when she mentioned Joe's stack of porn.

"Of course not," both gasped.

"Then why would you want to be like a man?"

"We're not saying—"

"—Oh, trust me, I know exactly what you're saying," Mug interrupted. "Like I tell the women I work with, I don't know why they'd want to walk around with something between their legs that controls their mind when they can be in charge of giving birth to, and raising, the type humans we want to see in the world!"

Both women smiled and looked at each other. Carmela then cleared her throat. "Wow, that was beautiful, exactly what we're looking for."

"Oh yeah honety chile," Mug said. "I keeps it real! So when am I going to be on Oprah?"

Mug called Mother back. "Chile, guess who just knocked on my door!"

"Who?"

"Oprah Winfrey!"

Mother didn't reply. Her mouth was open but no words came out.

"Well, not Oprah herself," Mug admitted. "She sent some of her people. They're going to do a feature on me."

"Why? For what," Mother asked, still highly skeptical.

"For what!?" Mug snapped offended. "Chile, for my long years and dedication working at Social Services. That's for what!"

"You've got to be kidding," Mother replied. "So, Oprah's people out-of-the-blue stopped by your house to talk to you?!"

"Sure did," Mug beamed. "They were here for a good while too! Someone told them about me and all the work I do for women. They nominated me for some kind of award."

"Wonder who that was," Mother muttered.

"You better stop that hatin'," Mug laughed. "You know God don't like ugly."

"Yeah, and that ain't all He don't like," Mother scoffed. She could've been specific but wasn't out to hurt Mug's feelings.

Truth was, Mug complained bitterly about the people she worked with, all the time. Every other week for as long as she'd known her...and they both moved on Gorgas Lane in 66' ...she cried about quitting social work. The same people supposedly awarding her, she often described as thimbles and tumblelinas, and the dirtiest of tags for women raking her spine was tarts and twats; gentile epithets compared to the tats she had for men.

Everyone on Gorgas Lane knew about Mug's troubles working in what they called the welfare office. No one could blame her for complaining either. From scavengers to government crooks, it was a rough place to work. Welfare workers had the worst clientele of any business. Every single last client was either dealing with some awful circumstances, or trying to get over. It took a beastly mentality to put up with the stuff that went on in that building. They completely understood the countless times she was out of work on long-term disability. Their only surprise was wondering why she hadn't been committed, since… that they knew of…she hadn't killed anyone.

"It probably was Ann who gave them my name," Mug offered. "She's always talking about how grateful she is to see me come in, and how when I quit, she was quitting too."

Mother disagreed. "I'll bet you my whole house it wasn't Ann," she chuckled.

"Why? Why you say that," Mug asked.

"Girl, first of all, I don't know how you got that much out of Ann. I never ever heard a complete a coherent sentence come out of that woman's mouth," Mother laughed. "Every time I've talked to her, I couldn't understand a word beyond 'hiya'!"

Mug chuckled. "Yeah chile, you might be right on that one."

"I know I'm right," Mother scoffed. "I just hope you got them people's names who got you to running your mouth, because I'd sure like to know what their angle was," Mother chuckled.

"Well, they gave me their business cards," Mug replied, a little less enthusiastic albeit. "Chile, at least they rolled over here proper," she suddenly remembered, a small redemption. "It was a pretty little blue BMW they parked in front of my door."

Mother froze. "Wait a minute," she said. "By chance, did one of these girls look half white and both look like they went to Girls' High?"

Mug froze too. Mother described the women perfectly.

18

Mug was hot. She went straight for Oscar's bottle of Johnnie Walker, the last bottle in the house. A few sips later her mood improved exponentially. It had been a while since her last drink. The ethanol went straight to her head.

Feet elevated, tall glass in hand, she was ready to go, sipping and humming, and humming and sipping... and waiting for someone to pick up the phone and tell her who nominated her, for what, and exactly when was she making her debut on Oprah. She was getting her money's worth out of Verizon on this day. Somebody was going to tell her something.

Mary Gonzales answered her call. At least that was the name Mug heard by the time her call was answered.

"Listen, 'yo' name ain't important," Mug yapped in the phone. "Who's name you want to know is mines!"

Taken aback but not knocked off any stools, Auriel...the woman's actual name, asked how she could help Mug.

"I need to know what kind of operation this is, and when am I scheduled to be on Oprah."

From this point forward the call was a bust. Auriel tried to get more out of Mug but used too many words, in too many accents, speaking way too fast for Mug to understand in her condition. By the time Auriel finished, the miscommunication had gone South both ways.

"Ma'am...ma'am...are you safe? Would you like for me to call 911," Auriel asked for the manyeth time.

"And put somebody on this damn phone that speaks plain English," Mug kept slurring back.

But this was as plain English as the call got when her daughter Leslie walked in the house to find her mother clearly off the wagon.

"Ma' who are you talking to," she asked, seeing Mug's short stumpy legs kicked up on the table, which meant her butt was completely off the chair and her head sandwiched between the seat and table base. She kind of looked like a roach, upside down on its back.

On the table was a tall empty glass, turned sideways, and an almost empty bottle of Johnnie Walker, cap off. Also on the table was Mug's cellphone, where Auriel continued crying, "ma'am... ma'am...are you still there!?"

Leslie picked up the phone and introduced herself, learning Auriel directed calls for women in trouble.

"Is your mom okay," she asked concerned. "We were trying to send help but couldn't trace the call."

"I think my mom will be fine," Leslie told the worried woman. "If she still wants to speak to someone she'll probably call back once she sobers up!"

19

Up and down Gorgas Lane neighbors talked about the Oprah story. Depending on who heard what, depended on the rumor told. Some heard Oprah herself visited Mug. Apparently, someone saw a stretch black Rolls taking up half the parking spaces on the block and assumed it belonged to the talk show diva. Others heard Mug was going to make an appearance on OWN. There was a debate about whether the episode was online or live. A few laughed about a late Halloween hoax pulled on Mug, some whispering about who they thought were involved. And there also was a gossip ring circulating that Oscar really beat Mug up, the reason two women from a women's advocacy group were dispatched. Supposedly they hid Mug in a women's shelter. Eventually one version reached Maxine, another one of the girls who lived on Gorgas Lane.

"Woman, have you and Oscar been in here going at it again?"

If any two of the girls were more alike in personality, but polar opposite in looks, it was Maxine and Mug. Maxine was a tall woman, almost six feet, and Mug barely five feet. Maxine was on the slender side, kind of resembling an ostrich around the legs, and from the neck up. Mug, of course, looked exactly as her husband tagged her. But of those differences, both women were exactly alike in one way. Neither hesitated to stand their ground.

These two could move an attitude from 0 to 10 going straight street level in Nano seconds. Once Mug opened her home to her sister-in-law, one of Oscar's sisters, and for days the pair were like Thelma and Louise best friends. Both loved Tyler Perry's Madea, and only used Miracle Whip as their mayonnaise. They had a similar fashion sense. If it fit, was clean, and covered the three V's, they'd wear it. They drank anything with alcohol in it, and could talk for hours. There wasn't a topic they didn't disagree on, except but one. Her sister-in-law didn't vote, because she thought all politicians were douches.

Say what!? Their ancestors had died fighting for their right to vote. Mug kicked her sister-in-law O-U-T. Threw her out in the streets. Not in her house. Everyone breathing under her roof were required to vote when they came of age.

Maxine was the same. She loved every one of her five children she brought in the world. Would give them the shirt off her back and go without if it came to it. But be damned if she was going to pretend she loved her oldest daughter's so-called husband. First of all, the husband was a woman. And Maxine wasn't walking nobody down an aisle, going along with a farce, just because her child and the she-man were sick in the head.

Now, the issue would have remained at the civil five level had not the she-man taken her all the way to ten. Maxine actually could give two damns about who, or what, her child liked hopping in bed with. Bottom line, a woman was a woman, like a dog would always be a dog.

Not in her lifetime was she going to start switching up hard scientific facts, none of it she quoted from any Bibles. She was talking straight up 101 common sense. Hell, what was she going to do if her next child came home talking about she liked walking upside down on her hands? For seven decades she'd been walking on her feet. She was like an old dog, too grounded to learn new tricks.

Unfortunately, her daughter hadn't spoken to her since she and the she-man fell out, and supposedly got married, of course a wedding Maxine missed.

But many years passed since either Maxine or Mug put their street level attitudes on full display, though in no way did this mean that Mug would stand for Oscar putting his hands on her, in any fashion, at any age, and in any day.

"I wish a mo'fo would," Mug replied, standing in front of a mirror teasing her hair. They were about to join the other girls at a new black owned bar and grill that recently opened ostensibly at Vera's invite. A dignitary was going to be there. A dignitary who of course was good friends with Vera, the reason Mug was doing a last-minute check making sure every strand of her hair was in place.

"I can't hit him like I used to," Mug went on, playing with her hair, checking both sides, "but I still know how to sit him down. He don't fool around with me," she said spinning around and whipping out a handheld mirror to check out the back too.

"Well, two women came by my house asking about you and Shugga, as if y'all was hiding some kind of abusive relationship," Maxine pried.

Instantly Mug pulled the handheld mirror away from her face. "Was one of 'em long headed and the other nappy headed, and driving a shiny BMW?"

"I didn't see the car, but they said they were with some women's group investigating abused women."

"Girl, don't pay them no mind. I don't know what them Karens are up to but they came by here, and Mother said they came by her house too!"

"Well, what's up with Shugga? I hear she left her job and moved to Africa to marry a rich Nigerian she met online!?"

"Ain't my business. Shugga 69-years old," Mug replied grabbing her coat. "God bless her If she want a Mandingo. God bless her... and God help her too," she cackled, cracking up laughing with Maxine who burst out laughing.

"Chile, I don't ever think Shugga been with a man," Maxine snickered.

"Well, apparently she's with one now," Mug replied, stepping outside with Maxine a step ahead. "I just hope she's enjoying it, because it'll be such a shame if all that testosterone goes to waste."

"Yeah, guess we won't be able to tease her about them tight butt-cheeks no more," Maxine chuckled, puffs of frosty air following them to the curb where they hopped in her car.

20

The atmosphere in the Platinum Grille was lively when Maxine and Mug arrived. The dining area was full and the waiting area packed, though it was the bar that caught their full attention.

"One drink," Maxine threw over her shoulder, warning Mug. "I don't like fighting my friends, but I will carry your little ba'hind right on out of here if you act up."

But there was no need for the warning. Mug was hardly embarrassing herself. Not when she spotted the mayor among a large entourage, about to hook his ample lips on a glass he held in his hand. She didn't miss a beat. She hurried up to him and demanded a hug on the spot.

"Oh Lord! Jesus! Trouble just done showed up," Myrtle belted, followed by Vera slipping between the mayor and Mug.

"Behave Jules, this is the mayor," Vera cooed, silenced by Mug whipping her head around, looking her up and down.

"You don't think I know that!? I know who he is," she shrieked. "Who can miss them lips. Almost knocked me over the minute I stepped foot in this place!"

"You so lucky," Mug said looking up at the mayor, and not at his face, but directly into his mouth. "Boy, if had I married you, I would've long ago sucked them things off your face!"

One of the men in the entourage almost sprayed the mayor in the face with his drink. He had to cover his mouth and turn his head to laugh.

"Alright," Vera said, stepping in between the mayor and Mug, about to intervene, except the mayor stopped her.

"She's fine," he said, barely moving his lips, almost barely making a sound.

"Y'all here that," Mug swung around cheering and beaming. "The mayor said I'm fine!" She danced around him, the top of her head reaching just about at his elbow. Stealing much of the spotlight, especially the mayor's attention, she yik-yakked about every grievance she had with the operations of the city.

"I want to know what's up with all this going green mess," she asked. Without waiting on his reply she told him there wasn't a thing no one could do about saving the ozone, but there was something he could do about her having to drag a thousand bags of garbage to the curb. "Makes no sense," she fussed.

"You need to make Oscar put down that bottle and take the trash out," Maxine teased. "Especially since you say he ain't good for much else."

"Yeah, she oughta be thanking him for at least creating jobs—"

"—Why," Mug snapped at Mother. "I already have a job! I had a job long before he was elected! And whoever he created these new jobs for, they need to come separate my trash, since I obviously ain't the one getting paid to do it!"

"Yeah, but it is a pain in the ba'hind sorting our trash," Myrtle agreed with Mug. "Especially when I see guys dumping it all on the same trash truck!"

"Girl, tell me about it," Mug fussed. "And can't nobody tell me them trash trucks is separating all that mess!"

The mayor smiled and nodded. "But how do you like them smooth streets," he asked.

Mug thought for a minute, unlike Myrtle who didn't miss a beat.

"If you're talking about the Drives, I'll give you credit. But take a trip down the north side of Broad Street sometime around February," she chuckled. "One time I hit a pothole so deep the jolt almost wired my jaws shut."

"Damn," Mother muttered, "just our luck."

"Yeah, maybe she'll fall off a stool and the knockers will finish the job smothering her," Maxine chuckled, turning on her heels and with Mother walking to where Vera sat at the end of the bar, one leg crossed over the other and batting the acrylic lashes, talking with a man who looked like he was working on getting to know her better.

"Look, this is a great city," the mayor replied to the two remaining girls. "You must admit many wonderful things have happened over the past few years—"

"—Oh, I love my city," Mug said cutting him off, though interrupted by Myrtle commanding far more attention with the girls she had hoisted up, front and center, especially by one man in the entourage trying to read between her lines.

"Yeah, that stadium is beautiful," she belted, pulling out a long Virginia Slim, headed for the door. "Now only if them Eagles can win us a Superbowl!" And off she strutted to the door, followed by laughter and the one man in the entourage who had been checking her out.

But while the crowd gnawed on her comment, tossing their two cents in the ring, Mug sort of pulled the mayor's ear to the side.

Looking at him earnestly, this time directly in his eye, she shared her one overriding concern. "Look, I understand men did us wrong, but what is up with all these women's groups sproutin' up, trying to turn all of us into victims? They make us look weaker."

The mayor tilted his head, obviously in the dark on this issue. And really, this had only recently become an issue for her as well. Because of the fraudsters who showed up at her door, she was getting hassled by her girls and neighbors. People were whispering and spreading rumors about her. And some people at her job were asking questions, namely her bosses. But more so than all of that, those girls really pissed her off jacking up her hopes to meet Oprah, only to dash that dream, plus turn her into a victim...which she was not.

"Somebody needs to look into these two women going up and down Gorgas Lane spreading lies and rumors. I don't want to have to hurt nobody, 'cause if I do, it'll be on your watch!"

21

And that did it! Though Mug, nor any of the other girls knew it at the time, but they had rapped on ears with teeth.

Between Vera's chats with Barry, President of Programs at the Board of Education, and Mug's conversation with the mayor, and a half dozen oddball incidents where one of the girls names kept popping up, none more so than Mug's and Mother's names, it was no longer pure gossip floating around the city. Prickly conversations had taken place and important people were asking damning uncomfortable questions.

What authority did anyone have to order police to interrogate Julia Davies, and just who was Julia Davies to begin with? Why was her home surrounded and where did the resources to investigate average citizens missing less than 48 hours come from? Not only was this Georgia Turner, who nobody knew... other than her close family and friends... out-of-pocket less than 48 hours, but she was on vacation for cripes sake! And yet the real omniscient question was, who in the devil were the two women impersonating reporters, fallaciously reporting on these extraneous matters?

This was what Peter Flynn, the president of KYL, wanted to know. "I don't know what's going on, but I'm hearing some very disturbing accusations about two young women, which if this stuff I'm hearing is true, then we have two people on staff acting well outside the scope of their employment," he fired off at Rita Shivers, who in relay communicated those career-ending offenses to Marsha Woodward.

"And just so you understand the wraths of hell about to rain down on all of us," Rita seethed, "some very important people are quite invested in the outcome of this situation."

No doubt. Marsha tried to swallow, except nothing worked. She needed to find her on switch, and flip it in the up position, to turn on the veins that talked to her brain, that told her vocal chords when to speak and what to say.

Rita said she could lose her job, a given. But in addition to losing her job, she could end up on the unemployment line for the rest of her natural life, blackballed from finding work so much as in a prison. She as well might be chipped, monitored and harassed by the dozens of people who were offended, insulted, harmed or pained in any way by the actions of...and she moved an arm to read two names scribbled in the notes on her calendar... "Carmela Moore and Julianna Price."

Marsha thought she'd gotten a second lease on life when Rita released her and she returned to her office, wobbly kneed, hair frizzed up looking like a Richard Simmons afro, and heart beating irregularly. There had to be a conspiracy at work. She was so sure of it.

Carmela and Julianna weren't that stupid. These were college educated young women. They came from hardworking, respectable families. They lived in the suburbs. They bragged about staying south of Broad & Market. The only time they saw the north part of the city was from the highway, traveling up 76 to get home, or to check in with her, who worked on the Main Line. There was no way that two nice young ladies cut from this decent cloth, who would rather cut off their legs than venture to the Northwest parts of the city, and on Gorgas Lane no less, would knock on strangers doors like used insurance salesmen, impersonating journalists on behalf of Oprah, of all people!

By the time Carmela and Julianna got to the main office it looked like Marsha had parted ways with God and settled on recruiting for the devil.

"You girls had so much promise here," she said. "Within a year's time I fully expected both of you to be working on a news desk."

"And so now you tell us," Julianna muttered.

"What did you say," Marsha hissed.

"But it was you who told us getting solid good stories takes imagination, and guts," Carmela spoke up. "I actually think we've accomplished that."

Initially Marsha had no words, since having her hearing checked at the moment was not an option. "Look, I want a full outline on whatever you were working on before you leave," Marsha herself replied, in lieu of what the other Marsha wanted to say. And raising a hand before Carmela or Julianna spoke, she finished.

"Now, I'm leaving today at seven, which means I need your notes on my desk no later than 6:59. If I don't have those notes before then, God help you, because I am not going down alone!"

It was 10:03am when Marsha gave that terse order, and 10:23am when she finished reading off a long list of individuals, each wanting a quart of their blood, and a head a piece. And she included herself as one of the sought-after donors. By 11:01am Carmela and Juliana were in the BMW pulling together all they had. By 11:19am they were back in Marsha's office, turning over everything. Notes, interviews, recordings, phone conversations, emails...everything.

And that's how the three; Carmela, Julianna, and Marsha made a sisterhood pact and came up with a pilot they felt would squash the rumors, save lots of faces, spare KYL a likely expensive lawsuit and bring many smiles to many women.

"Told you this was going to work," Carmela chuckled, her and Julianna back in the BMW.

"Oh please," Julianna yawned rolling her eyes. "We dodged a bullet and you know it!"

22

Mug had just swung her legs off the bed, dangling about a foot and a half above the floor as she reached back patting the comforter, feeling around for the TV remote when the phone started ringing.

"Who in the devil could this be calling this early," she muttered to herself. Wasn't even 8 o'clock. It had to be a telemarketer because no one begged harder for a butt whipping than them.

Instead of reaching for the remote, which took great effort to abandon, given her eagerness to get the channel off Judge Joe Brown, she instead went for her glasses on the nightstand, to figure out who was calling.

"Damn!" She needed more glasses for the glasses she tried to read the number on caller ID through. The random string of numbers appeared to be coming from New Zealand, or a place even further. Just for making her look she started to pick up the phone and slam it back down, when it dawned on her, it could've been Shugga calling from the Motherland.

Lawd! Shugga could've been calling, stranded, done in by the African Kings and Queens, reaching out for help. Not that she could do much from where she was, but she was a damn good listener...and this she wanted to hear.

"Hello?" she snapped into the phone; in case it was a telemarketer. Contrary to the insinuation, she liked talking to them. She loved appeasing people looking for butt whippings. The verbal butt whippings were her favorite. She didn't get as winded.

"May I speak to Julia Davies, please?"

"This is she."

Suddenly, like a red rose yawning and opening its eyes, a tiny voice sifted through the phone. "Mrs. Davies, my name is Marsha Woodward. I'm the executive producer for a prime-time program, calling to find out if you would be open to doing an interview with us?"

Alright now, this was where the quote occurred to Mug. Fool her once, shame on her. Fooling her twice wasn't gonna happen.

"Lady, if you aren't Oprah, which you just told me you aren't, I don't have a thing to say!"

Marsha paused, taking a quick breath before speaking. From the detailed notes Carmela and Julianna collected, she knew Mug was a pit of fire. This was a woman who'd give her a tongue-lashing and end the call within the amount of time it took most to think I, let alone pronounce it.

"I can't get you Oprah, but maybe the mayor might convince you," she quickly got out. The offer stopped Mug dead in the middle of an impending tongue-lashing.

"Now, I know it's early, and hope I didn't wake you, so I'll give you my telephone number and address. You can call me at your convenience, if and when you'd like to do an inter—"

"—I don't need to call back," Mug said cutting her off. "But I'm not talking to no stranger over the phone. Just give me your address and I'll drop by after I get off work."

"Well, I was thinking about saving you a trip because—"

"—Aww no sugar," Mug replied. "That's where ya' wrong. I don't need no favors. What's the address?"

"We're on City Line but our office closes at—"

"—Oh yeah, I'll have to catch the 44. Let me talk to my kids first, because I can't afford to get stranded on a hoax!"

"Mrs. Davies, I can assure you this isn't a hoax—"

"—Umm hmm," Mug hummed. "That's what the other Karens told me," she snapped.

"Karens?" Marsha echoed confused.

"Yeah, them two girls that have been harassing my neighbors, with their lyin' ba'hinds!"

"Oh yes," Marsha sighed. "I did hear about that," she replied. "And trust me, the mayor got on my case about it too.

I hope you will accept my sincere apology. That's why I have to make sure this is done right."

Mug smiled on that remark. The 'ole mayor really came through for her. "Tell me something," she started, smiling at a far-off thought. "What does his lips look like?"

23.

"Wake up woman! I got some news to tell you," Mug shouted excitedly into the phone.

"Chile, I've been up since four this morning," Mother said switching the phone to the other ear as she rolled over, propping herself up on one elbow.

"What's wrong with you? You've been up eatin' them Fritos, haven't you?"

They both laughed, Mug laughing hardest. She knew it was about the only thing that kept Mother up all night.

"Chile, my heart has been so heavy," Mother confided. "I don't know what it is...but something about Shugga—"

"—Girl, that's why I'm calling," Mug interjected. "Guess who hooked us up!"

"What? Who?"

"Lushes, Girl!"

"Who?"

"Our mayor!" Mug exclaimed like Mother should've caught the description right away. "He found them lyin' heffas and had some woman call here to apologize!"

"Wait...what!?" Mother repeated.

"Chile, you just better get right," Mug cackled, excited ten levels above her usual, and she had experienced a lot of excitement in her lifetime. Once when she hit the jackpot in Trump Towers and was put up in the penthouse, and another time when she busted out the windows in Oscar's car, thinking he was about to give some woman a ride home from a club where he had been showing out all night.

"They're putting us on a reality show," Mug exclaimed.

"Woman please!" Mother chuckled. "And leave my mayor and his lips alone."

"I'm serious," Mug replied. "This woman—" and Lord, she'd already forgotten the dern woman's name! "A producer just called," she inserted for the name she'd forgotten. "I'm meeting with her, over there on City Ave, to set it up. All of us are going to be on it!"

"But why would they put the two of us on TV," Mother chuckled. "I mean, other than for mug shots?"

"Girl, not just us," Mug explained. "...I gave her all of our names...mines, yours, Vera's, Myrtle's...all of us. They want to hear our perspectives on womanhood, and motherhood, and how we made it through them awful times."

"What awful times," Mother protested. "Chile, back in the day were some of the best days of our life!"

And this was true. Just about every day was a cause to celebrate. Between the backyard birthday parties, the cookouts, the holiday dinners and gatherings, there was hardly more than the rare funeral when someone was noticeably down. And even then, they didn't stay down long. Depending on who was in the casket, everybody's mood lifted shortly after the casket was closed. Thus, true tragedies were rare.

"Chile, you remember Mr. Charlie's funeral," Mother chuckled. Few would forget that home-going. Mr. Charlie, his soul resting in peace, lived a long regular life. He left the world, leaving 11 children and countless grand, great-grand and great-great grand. Not a one of his surviving relatives dropped a tear, though there were tears galore at that service.

Mug started it, when one of the great-great-grand, a child of about five, egged on by his grandmother, got to playing a song on a violin for his great-granddaddy. Grandmother Lo guided the lopsided head child to the altar and pushed him in front of the mic. That's what started the moaning. The child's head was shaped like a disfigured lightbulb. There were lumps all over the boy's head. And then he blew into the violin. The sound that initially came out was bad, but got worse. And even worse. By the time the child put the instrument down, someone had to help Mug up from beneath the pew. She'd gotten stuck after falling off the bench she laughed so hard.

"Lord Chile, me and Lo still aren't speaking," Mug laughed.

"Chile, I'm surprised Mr. Charlie didn't get up out that casket and throw that child in it! Lo oughta' known better than to embarrass that boy like that," Mother laughed, reaching for her nightstand, over a pharmacy of sinus aides to grab a tissue.

"I think the boy now lives in that house," Mug said. "He and that girl he is in there living with tore that house down."

"You mean, finished tearing down," Mother added as she wiped her eyes. "Lo wasn't nothing but a big put on, leaving that old man in that raggedy house, crying them bucket of tears at the funeral."

"Chile, I was surprised she showed up at the funeral at all," Mug said. "Charlie must've left some money behind."

"That's why when I die, I told my kids to bury me butt naked," Mother chuckled. "I want y'all to prop me up on my knees with my ba'hind facing the congregation...and make sure my ba'hind is good and greased. I want it nice and shiny 'cause I don't like no ashy ba'hinds!"

"Aww Girl," Mug howled. "You think somebody gonna pay ten thousand to have folk kiss your ba'hind!"

"I know I wouldn't," Mug continued, chuckling. The comeback lost Mother for a second. "Shucks them glorified undertakers charged Max a thousand dollars just to put Herbert's pants on! Remember that," Mug asked laughing.

Suddenly Mother caught on. She remembered Maxine's father, Herbert, who according to legend the girls still laughed about, caused the funeral director issues trying to tape down his johnson. "Yeah, but we took care of our parents, just like we did our kids..."

...And this was true too. They took care of the children during the day, and partied at night. From one 4th of July to the next they celebrated all the holidays. Easter, Memorial's Day, Labor Day, Halloween, Thanksgiving, New Year's Eve... they recognized them all. One party for children, and one for them. Even sitting on the porch gossiping about rain ripping and running up and down the street was enjoyable. The best they could call awful was scoffing at the one remaining white man who lived across the street. He used to sit on his porch, yelling at their children for walking on what he called, 'his sidewalk'. But even that wasn't so awful. The old man was scared out of his wits. Apparently, he couldn't gather funds as quickly as the others who climbed aboard the white flight, running off to the suburbs. It was months after his cohorts fled before he scrounged up the dough he needed to escape his new black neighbors. Mother felt sorrier for him than she did their children.

"Chile, I'm not complaining," Mug chuckled. "Do you still have any of Richard Pryor's albums?"

"Do I," Mother cackled. "That man kept us all rolling on the floor," she added, snatching another tissue out of the tissue box. "It's probably what's wrong with people today," she said blowing her nose.

"Un hun..." Mug agreed. "They need to get off these high horses and live and laugh and love a little! That's why I liked what this woman that called here today was talking about. We got to teach these youngins about what being a woman and a mother really was like!"

24

When Myrtle got wind of the reality show, the first thing she did was pick up two fashion magazines while waiting in the supermarket checkout. "I have to be right," she teased with Vera, the fashionista who could talk fashion night and day.

"Mertie...girl," Vera started in her signature whine. "You going on the show?"

Myrtle really hadn't given a lot of thought to appearing on the show. She, like the other girls had received the invite, along with a ten-page standard contract, thereby more than just talk, but had reservations about being in spotlights that bright. Don't get her wrong, she liked looking good and being at the center of men's attention, but wasn't gunning to be a public spectacle.

"Chile, I don't know," Myrtle sighed. "I've got to read that contract!"

Vera didn't reply to Myrtle's comment. Her contract was laying, unopened, on a stack of mail. "Well, I've got to get some of this weight off these hips," she sang instead. "Girl, I'm starting to look and walk just like Gayle!"

Gayle was Vera's mother, a woman with huge hips that moved like a giraffe with a wombat rear end, trying to switch. Her mother was no longer alive, but everyone used to laugh at her walk, swaying like a hula-hoop.

"Me too," Myrtle belted. "I was in Saks the other day, trying on this dress...Lord Chile...found out I can't do nothing with anything under a 22!"

Vera squealed laughing. "So, you can't get in a 22 Mertie," she cooed.

"Nope. Me and 22 no longer friends," Myrtle replied.

"But they're not making clothes like they used to," Vera said. "I can't find anything I like. The stuff they're making nowadays look so cheap."

"I noticed that," Myrtle replied. "Chile, I had to asked the salesgirl if they were no longer working with the same buyers! And I'm talking Saks," she emphasized hammering another exclamation onto the end of her point.

"I guess fashion went out when all the good stores started closing down. Strawbridge's, Wannamaker's, Gimbels...all of them are gone," Vera said.

"Chile, Gimbels closed down years ago! It used to be my go-to when I couldn't get downtown... before the kids started wearing high-top sneakers and Jordache jeans," Myrtle huffed.

"Oh, I had a pair of Jordache jeans," Vera smiled thinking back. "Girl, I used to wear the heck out of them bad boys!"

"Me too," Myrtle belted. "Sassoon, Vanderbilt, Calvin Klein...I wore 'em all! Of course back then I was wearing a size 8," she huffed.

"Couldn't tell us nothing, huh," Vera continued smiling. "And just think, size 2's back in the day was like wearing an 8 today."

"Oh Lord, Jesus Veer! Do we have to go there!?"

Vera chuckled. It was a painful memory for her as well. She wasn't far off from a 22 herself, what gratefully was the new 8 in 2013. "I remember when I was a kid and Mother made our clothes," she said, switching memories.

"Mother," Myrtle shouted. "When did Mot—"

"—Not Mother Washington," Vera corrected. "I'm talking about Gayle, making even our coats. But I haven't seen a fabric store in years either," she sighed.

"Oh, I was about to say," Myrtle chuckled. "Because the only thing our Mother seems to make, is mess!"

"Aww..." Vera cooed. "Mother was just worried about Shugga, that's all."

"And Shugga, have you heard any more about her?"

"No," Vera replied. "All I know is I think she married an African. A rich one," she added. "I think Shirley said they're coming back this way around the first of the year."

"Oh Lord, Jesus Christ," Myrtle belted. "What kind of rich man would want to marry Shugga's crazy ba'hind?"

Vera squealed again, eyes closed and holding the note like she had a song deep in her heart. Each time Myrtle both belted and said 'oh Lord', her voice, heavy when she so much as sighed, reverberated like thunder had struck.

"Leave my friend alone," Vera giggled. "Ain't nothing wrong with Shugga."

"The lie you tell," Myrtle huffed, picking up her Virginia Slims and pulling out one long white cigarette. "The girls are gonna have a field day if she bring that man back here," she said, lighting the cigarette and taking a nice long draw.

"You think the girls are going to get on Shugga about that man, Mertie?"

"You seriously want my answer?" Myrtle replied, smoke billowing around her head.

"Oh, the girls will be alright," Vera giggled. "They did fine with the mayor."

"Yeah well, I sure won't be fooling around with the girls, and Shugga and the African on the same show," Myrtle shot back, taking another draw off the cigarette and exhaling. "Mother is trouble enough, but add Max and Mug and I hardly want to be the one!"

Vera howled. Myrtle definitely hammered the nail on the head with that one. The three M&M's were like a full house. Throw in Shugga and it was a Royal Flush!

25

Shirley called Mother a few days after returning from London, which happened to be a few days before Thanksgiving. The show was scheduled to be taped December 16th. She didn't yet know this, but was about to find out.

"Girlfriend, I'ma stop by Thursday, to bring you and Joe some dinner. I got a recipe for chitt'lings that can't be beat," she said excited. "Girl, these intestines are hot!"

"Chile, I so much appreciate it," Mother replied. "Cause I was about to order take out from the Soul Food Kitchen," she laughed.

"Oh no, you don't want to be fooling around in them greasy fold up spoons," Shirley chuckled. "After you taste these chitterlings, you'll never look at another greasy spoon!"

Every Thanksgiving Shirley cooked, be it for a hundred people, or in this case, for only Joe and Mother. She got a hold of a chitterling recipe from a woman she met in London ...ahem, native of Louisiana...that she couldn't wait to get feedback.

"Well, Joe and I will be here waiting...since everybody seem like they crossed Thanksgiving off their calendars!"

The offbeat remark caught Shirley by surprise. Mother didn't have to sit home with no Thanksgiving meal. Even if their kids were consumed with their new families and lives, there still was Mug, and Maxine, and Myrtle, and plenty of other friends and neighbors on Gorgas Lane who would gladly include them in their holiday plans.

"Well, what's Mug and them doing," Shirley wondered aloud. It was almost sacrilegious not to eat a proper pilgrim meal on Thanksgiving.

"Chile, I don't know what Maxine is doing, but Myrtle said she was going over to her sister's house, and I'm hardly squeezing up in Mug's little shoebox with the mayor and everybody else she said she invited."

"The mayor," Shirley asked taken aback.

"Yeah Girl, Mug done got in the mayor's ear and ended up getting all of us on this show. And you know how it is when you get to running your mouth about how you're about to blow up. Everybody comes out the woodwork thinking you already are getting paid."

Truth be told, all of their houses were built around the same time, using the same 1800 square foot blueprint, probably built by the same man too. Well, that being all of them except Vera who lived in a large white house at the base of a hill in Blue Bell, and Elaine who lived on top of all success's letters in an Arizona mansion. The point being, none of them exactly lived in a shoebox. While a hundred people in 1800 square feet of space would be a little tight, they had entertained large crowds before, and every time Mother was there.

But Shirley shook her head confused, hearing one small part. "All y'all were on a show?"

"No! The show hasn't happened yet," Mother replied. "They're taping it in a couple of weeks. You will be on it too."

"Oh no I'm not," Shirley retorted, already convinced. "I don't know nothing about a show," she added. All she got when talking to one of the girls, was questions about London, and the triplets, and of course them wanting to know what Shugga was up to.

"Well, you were invited," Mother said. "Didn't you get the contract?"

"A contract," Shirley asked. "What kind of contract?"

"It was in a big white envelope," Mother replied. "You can't miss it. It has KYL's logo all over it."

"Ump," Shirley hummed. She'd seen that piece of mail, but put it aside with the junk mail. "But how did Mug get to talk to the mayor!?"

"Vera invited us to one of her mixers...over there at the new black owned restaurant that just opened...and of course the mayor and his entourage was there, which you know how Mug is..."

"Oh Lord," Shirley sighed. "I bet she was all in that man's mouth," she chuckled.

"Girl, and that's putting it mildly!"

"But what kind of show is this supposed to be?"

"One of them reality type shows," Mother replied. She wasn't sure. She never really looked into things, beyond halfway listening to hearsay.

"You mean like Jerry Springer!?"

"Girl, No! It's one of them PBS type news shows that interviews women's groups."

"Since when has Mug joined a woman's group," Shirley scoffed.

Mother couldn't answer that, because Mother didn't know much beyond she hadn't been left out. She may have not been flying anywhere to be on TV, but at least she was going to be on TV. That was good enough for her, unless something better popped up.

"All I know is we're answering questions about what it was like for us as women and mothers back in the day."

"Aww shucks!" Shirley fussed. "I'm getting sick and tired of these women out here acting like being a woman is something new. They act like they got here by themselves! Don't they have a mother or somebody to explain that stuff to them?"

"Ain't that the truth," Mother agreed. "We learned from our mothers, like they learned from their mothers," she sort of fussed too. "The thing that really gets me are the ones running around whining about being a single mother like it's everybody else's fault. Shucks, nobody put a gun to their head and made them get pregnant...and have that baby!"

"Chile, we got one on the job who think she supposed to get special treatment when she need time off," Shirley huffed. "Mother's Day they were going to make me work for her, like I don't have children who might want to take me out! Shucks, I paid my dues! Being an empty-nester is my reward! I earned that!"

"We sure did," Mother agreed. "Some nerve."

"Shoot...yeah Girl, I told them, ain't nobody cut me no slack when my child was in the hospital and I needed time off! She'll figure it out, just like I had to!"

"But we did have better daycare back then—"

"—Unt unn!" Shirley retorted. "Wasn't no daycare back then!"

"Well, I mean we had more reliable sitters. We looked after each other's children."

"And didn't put our parents in nursing homes either," Shirley chimed in.

"Ooo Girl, yeah! Only white people did that."

"Yeah, but can you blame 'em? Shucks, we took care of their kids... nursed them and all, " Shirley chuckled. "They had to expect that! I would've thrown their trifling ba'hinds in an old age home too!"

"But that's what get me about our kids. Now they trying to be like white people, and here we took care of their butts," Mother scoffed.

"Yeah, we were a village," Shirley agreed. "But today everybody is so spread out. I don't know half the neighbors around here anymore."

"Girl, did you see that house on the 300 block? Where those Jamaicans moved into?"

"Chile, I don't go that way no more. I stay off Ardleigh," Shirley huffed.

"Well, the next time you do, you're going to think you're on the Ivory Coast," Mother chuckled. "Chile, they got a canoe out on the front lawn. And it's painted yellow and green."

"I've seen it," Shirley scoffed. "Why you think I stopped going that way!"

"Chile, I had to do a double-take," Mother continued, getting to her real point. "Thought for sure we were on that river, remember that village in Africa?"

"I'm trying not to," Shirley replied. "I still get sea sick thinking about it."

Mother laughed. Shirley was a strong swimmer, a lot stronger than her anyway, but looked like she was seeing her last days when they took that trip to Africa and decided to tour the Ivory Coast...by canoe. It was one of the funniest trips they'd ever taken. Mother and Mug had their mouths open the entire trip, laughing at Shirley who after the river excursion mostly stayed in the hotel...calling herself touring the Motherland looking through a pair of binoculars, from their room.

"Yeah, you're laughing," Shirley went on, but I bet you won't find me on Jerry Springer!"

"Oh Girl, it's not that kind of reality show. The taping is going to be done in a studio out there on City Ave," Mother said.

"I know where KYL is," Shirley shot back. "And still, you won't find me in there embarrassing myself fooling around with y'alls crazy ba'hinds!"

26

By Black Friday, buzz about the program buzzed up. Not only were the girls talking about their appearance on the talk show, but advertisements about the broadcast were appearing nationwide. [KYL presents Real Women - Documentary Airs - 60Mins. - (Channel 101) - Eight close friends discuss relationships, faith and secrets.]

Maxine hit the ceiling when she saw this.

"Ma', what kind of secrets y'all gonna be telling," her daughter asked, looking at her with one brow raised.

This was Maxine's youngest daughter asking, the child who spent a year explaining to jurors she wasn't running a Ponzi scheme, but a su-su club. She ended up getting a slap on the wrist and a cagey cue to keep a low profile. She definitely didn't want this experience rehashed for public viewing. Not only were there people still feeling cheated by her su-su club, she was a real estate broker for Mellon Bank. Plus, years ago when she was a child, she read Maxine's diary and found out her mother wasn't so clean either.

"I don't know," Maxine replied through gritted teeth, "but I'm soon about to find out!"

She didn't bother dialing Shirley. Though Shirley could be a two-faced somebody, she heard through the grapevine Shirley tore up the contract. So she called Mother, Shirley's two-faced sidekick, Ms. Innocent stirring the pots… good at smiling in people's faces and talking behind their backs, and then laying low in cuts when the heat got hottest. Case in point, how this whole thing got started in the first place!

Maxine wasn't buying the sweet innocent routine. This was a shady wench she planned to shake like a fruit tree.

"Maxine, I don't have any secrets," Mother replied. "And I surely don't know anything about any of you that no one else doesn't already know," she said concerned. Though Maxine was on the phone, one wrong word could bring the hostility to her front door in one stride.

"Well, why am I hearing some secrets are going to be told on this show?"

"Huh?" Mother had no idea what Maxine was referring to. She hadn't seen the announcement.

"I'ma send you a text and show you what I'm talking about!"

Mother waited for the text, her hands shaking as she switched screens. Good Lord, please don't let her accidentally hang up on Max. The woman would swear she did it on purpose when never in her life would she knowingly do or say anything bad about her friend.

"I'ma tell you right now," Maxine continued while Mother read the text. "I will go off up in that bitch if anything comes out about me or my family! Y'all gonna think we on 'beat a friend's ass' if I hear some nonsense," and she wasn't laughing. She called Mug too, about to put that same heat in her ear.

"Whoa... what the hell," Mug started, sitting up on her sofa. She was off the wagon again, and not the bottle wagon. Unless provoked, she was a humble woman. She didn't care for boasting and bragging, and hated people who acted high and mighty...alas, her issue somewhat with Vera.

But she did like nice things, and especially nice people, alas again, where Vera rubbed off on her in a good way. She also loved the mayor, and not in a salacious way, but in a respected way of idolizing popular luminaries. She would give her arm or, okay, so maybe her first born, to stand on a mountain and be Shero of the universe. In other words, she liked the idea of being liked, or looked up to. That's how she got pranked the first time, and talked into doing an interview the second time. So, being off the wagon meant she had slipped into that hypocritical gray space she often scorned.

"I don't know what you're reading," Mug started, "but the only topics we'll be discussing, are our perspectives about being women and mothers, and trust me, I got a lot to say!"

Maxine might've been bigger…and a whole lot tougher, but Mug was hardly one to back down. She wasn't like Mother and Shirley, scared of controversary, and indeed she had a lot to say. A whole lot.

Mug got to snapping her neck, moving her head, eyes, hands and just about every part of her body describing exactly what was on her agenda. "I already told them, I ain't no victim," she fussed, sober as the Sahara. "These women running around whining about being women, having the nerve to want to be men, ain't me!

…I told them," she raved on, eyes closed as she caught her next wind about to dial things up to ten, "all that crap that happened to Bill while he was in office, better not happen to Barack! I am sick and tired of all these Paula's and Monica's and Anita's running around here ruining good men's careers playing victims. Shit! They got a mouth! They know how to say no and move on! They messing it up for all women, exactly like them burning bras hussies did!"

Mug continued on, hardly the end of all she had to say, but was enough for Maxine who had nothing to add, or subtract from the verbal whipping. Though she did vote, she wasn't a politicking type woman. But as Mug so aptly convinced her, if she had something to say, it definitely had nothing to do with any of her business. Like it or not, Mug didn't run around talking about stuff she wouldn't shove right back in the horse's mouth. That was real talk. Couldn't fault her for that.

27

But just in case, and for good measure to enforce the message... Maxine called Myrtle too.

"Oh Lord Jesus," Myrtle shouted the moment she heard Maxine's tiring voice and what sounded like a grueling long-winded rant a-coming. Eyes closed but facing the ceiling like any given Sunday when she was sitting in the front pew at Holy Cross Church, she called out for Jesus's help. "Lord, What Now!"

"Look, I just finished with Mother and Mug because I want everyone to know I will go off if we're going to be on that show telling secrets," Maxine explained, though a whole lot calmer than she had with either Mug, and especially Mother.

"Chile, what are you going on about? Nobody has any secrets," Myrtle said.

"That's not what I'm seeing on TV," Maxine huffed. "They're acting like it's going to be a cat fight on the show!"

"What!? Who's they?" Myrtle wanted to know.

"Here, let me send you the text I sent Mother." And she forwarded the text, a copied image of KYL's marketing campaign, created to dial up the tension well past extra to assure maximum excitement...a maneuver flawlessly executed, given Maxine had face-planted dead in the middle of the trap.

"Girl, they're puffing," Myrtle said after reading the text.

"Yeah, well...I'm going to be puffing too, if some mess comes out about me and mines," Maxine shot back.

"Did you read the contract," Myrtle asked.

Of course she hadn't. Like who among average readers, who rarely read more than street signs and headlines printed in bold font, bothered to read itsy-bitsy fine print?

"I gives not a damn about a contract," Maxine spat. "Y'all know me. I don't do foolishness! I'm not going to be cool if I hear any nonsense."

"Ugh, we got you on speed dial," Myrtle chuckled. She was born, raised and familiar with West Philly bad asses. Over her six and counting decades on earth, every last one of them spent living in Philadelphia, she met some of the toughest, and some of the meekest. Maxine fell somewhere in the middle, towards the lower end. She had a loud bark, but a heart of gold. Myrtle still remembered when she was sent to reformatory school after trying to punk a teacher. She cried all year, begging that same teacher to reinstate her so that she could go to school with the rest of them who didn't flip out every time someone did or said something that hurt her feelings. The child was pitiful.

"Just tell me one thing," Maxine huffed, almost out of steam. "There's only six of us, one who still hasn't signed the contract! So who are the other two?"

"I don't know," Myrtle replied, pulling out another cigarette. "Have you decided what you're wearing yet?"

"Yeah, I'm wearing boxing gloves," Maxine wryly chuckled. "I'm not kidding around," she raved on, going to her reservoir of feelings for more steam. "That's all these people do nowadays, is look for folk to exploit! Can't turn on the TV without seeing somebody on trial...the whole damn case played out for nothing but amusement and entertainment. Don't even need a jury no more. Shucks, all they need to do is set up an 800-number like they do for QVC and American Idol!

I'm telling you, I'm not going to be the one!"

"Ump," Myrtle wryly chuckled too, riled none by the rant. She had smoked half a pack of cigarettes and was opening a new pack by the time Maxine ran out of steam. "Look, if I was you," she laughed, "I'd read that contract, and tear it up and stay home if you don't agree with it. Whatever you do, I wouldn't embarrass myself," she warned. "You know everybody has a match..."

28

"Look, we all need to regroup," Vera was telling Myrtle upon catching wind of the fussing. "There's no reason for drama," she cooed, as if she was speaking to a child. "We are grown women who young women are looking up to. We need to represent," she said. "I think we oughta' to take Elaine up on her offer and visit her this weekend."

"Umm," Myrtle murmured. "I don't know about that."

Myrtle wasn't putting on. She kept a busy schedule. The upcoming weekend, when Elaine proposed the trip, she had a wedding and a funeral to attend. The following weekend was the taping, plus her sorority was holding their annual Christmas party. Christmas was the week after that, which she definitely had big plans for. She couldn't squeeze another thing on her jammed packed calendar, and certainly wasn't up for working her nerves to make time for a group of busy-body old friends, who she loved, but had no love for their fussing about nonsense.

Of course Mother, when she heard, had her bags packed before purchasing her airline ticket. She didn't need a special invite. "I'm taking off Thursday and Friday," she told Mug.

"Chile, I don't know if I feel like spending money that look funny, to sit in Elaine's palace all weekend," Mug chuckled. "I might have to Skype y'all!"

"Aww woman please," Mother laughed. "I've seen you throw two hundred on blackjack tables and walk away before the dealer counted the chips!"

This was true, but she did that once, when she had a drink too many.

"Yeah, and that's exactly why I'm staying my ba'hind home," Mug chuckled. "...I'd be losing money from the get go to go all the way out there. Elaine lives too far from a blackjack table!"

In the end the girls agreed to the trip, to include Myrtle who sent apologies to friends whose functions she was going to miss. They met up at the terminal, teasing and jostling with each other like old times, back in the day when they were throwing the cookouts and parties and fun functions they spent all week prepping for.

Maxine had calmed considerably. Like all of them, her hair and nails were freshly done, glowing from the crown of her head down to the jeweled Pradas she wore on her feet. She looked wide awake and refreshed, like she had spent all week pulling herself together.

At one point she did stand up and count them though. "Alright, unless my math is wrong, it is six of us here," she said. "Now, we know Shugga ain't going to be on the show, right?" and she looked around at the girl's oblivious expressions staring back at her. They knew what she was getting at but didn't know where she was going.

"She might," Shirley quietly muttered, turning her head the opposite way to smirk. "Y'all know Shugga," she chuckled wagging her leg. "It's no telling when or where she'll show up next."

"Lord, I can't wait to talk to Shugga," Vera said, steering the chit-chat away from wherever Maxine seemed to be going. "I miss 'ole Shugga," she chuckled. "It's never a dull moment when she's around."

Mug burst out laughing. "I remember that Halloween party when she came dressed as a pregnant nun. Y'all remember that?"

"Girl! Do we!?" Myrtle belted, coughing and patting her chest, moving flim from one side to the other. "I still have a picture of her...one with her hands folded, holding up the pillow cases...looking all innocent," she managed to say.

The girls remembered the party, as if it happened a day ago... Shugga dressed like a traditional Catholic sister, from head to toe. She was the talk of the party, though it was Mug and Oscar who shut down the night. They got to arguing, and then fighting, which was nothing new, except this night Mug was up on top of Oscar, straddling and punching him like a rogue cop before the guys could break up the fight. It was the first time any of them ever heard a man scream, begging her for his life.

"Girl, you beat that poor man like you saw the devil in him," Mother laughed.

"It took Joe, Chester, Father and Nathan to pull her off him," Maxine laughed too.

"Chile, I never knew I could really murder someone, until that night," Mug chuckled.

"No you couldn't have," Shirley said shaking her head. "People think that but—"

"—Oh yes I could have," Mug said swinging around to address Shirley. "Y'all don't know, but go ask Oscar if you don't believe me! He woke up the next day by the grace of God... and that steel vest he slept in that night," she scoffed rolling her eyes. "Pitchfork was sticking straight up out of his chest when I woke up," she added. "And it was still in his chest after I finished washing dishes..."

"Oh my God, Mug," Mother gasped.

"Well, you better thank God too," Myrtle scoffed. "They weren't giving death row inmates chin-straps back then."

The girls fell out laughing, shaking their heads. Maxine too.

They made it through one brow raising story, an x-ray scan, a pat down, a screaming toddler and one cranky flight attendant who threatened to ground the plane herself if the girls continued harassing passengers with their inappropriate jokes and loud laughing.

"I just want to know one thing," Maxine scoffed as they walked by the flight attendant who'd given her the most grief. "Where in the hell was she on September 11th!?!"

"What I don't get," Mug fussed as they headed to baggage claim. "Nobody gave a damn about that child screaming like a fool, looking over the seat at me like something Chucky upchucked," she huffed, softening up to add. "I mean, they now have hollerin' chirrens on planes, mothers with their titties out trying to feed them, drinks that costs an arm and a leg, fat ass cranky flight attendants, no food, filthy seats, dogs, cats and God only knows the hell in them carry-on bags, and yet folk have the nerve to draw the line at a little laughing!"

"But that was a cute little fat baby," Mother chuckled. "I wanted to bite them thighs."

"I would've," Mug scoffed. "...Had I thought about it."

Of course Mother wasn't speaking of hurting the child. She loved babies, kissing them between the folds in their neck and biting their chubby legs with her lips wrapped around her teeth. But not Mug. Mug hated hollering chirrens.

"Oool Mug," Vera squealed. "That's not nice," she chuckled. "I always wondered why Teddy used to pitch a fit

when I left him with you. Did you beat up my baby," she cooed.

"...Like a step-child," Mug chuckled.

"Mug, no you didn't," Vera whined. "You didn't beat up my baby," she chuckled too.

"Yes I did," Mug replied. "You had that boy spoiled rotten. Couldn't eat this, didn't want that, messing his pants with all them teeth in his head. Chile, I tore that fat tail up!"

The girls fell out laughing, knowing Mug was telling the absolute truth!

"That was a fat little something," Mother recalled. "And so sweet. I almost ate that baby up one night," she laughed.

"Yeah, but I bet you wouldn't want to get near them fat thighs now," Shirley chuckled.

"Oh yes I would," Mother laughed. "I haven't had that kind of fun in a while!"

That shut Shirley up, for a minute at least. She didn't subscribe to raunchy talking, unlike Vera who squealed, "oool Mother, y'all been sexually abusing my baby too?"

"Well, apparently it didn't hurt him," Mug chuckled. "He's doing alright now. I heard he's Head of the Water Department!"

"Frank Rizzo got him that job," Myrtle belted, huffing to keep up. "He started out working for Rizzo when he was about 10!"

Mug laughed out loud. "I remember that! Rizzo had that child running errands. I thought for sure he was going to end up a mobster!"

"Lord!" Myrtle suddenly belted, holding on to a wall trying to catch her breath. "Y'all go on. I'll meet y'all at baggage claim. I'ma catch a lift with one of the pall bearers."

The girls had stopped at least three times since they'd gotten off the plane, waiting for her. None of them were exactly in Marathon running shape, but they could walk more than a foot without having to catch their breath.

"Maybe now it might convince her to give up them cigarettes," Shirley whispered out the corner of her mouth.

"I doubt it," Mother whispered back. "She probably won't quit until they take out the other lung," she scoffed.

They left Myrtle waiting on the pall bearer, her word for a skycap, and kept walking and talking.

"I know one thing, traveling by plane is getting worse and worse," Mug scoffed.

"Almost like riding Greyhound," Maxine agreed.

"It's worse than Greyhound," Mug near shrieked.

"Why you think I said almost," Maxine shot back. "Between hollering babies and them nasty ass flight attendants, I'd rather walk!"

"Well, y'all can go on and walk. I'll take flying any day," Mother said, she who wouldn't pass up a trip, traveling all over the globe at least 15 times a year.

"Me too," Vera added, another frequent flyer. "You won't hardly catch me traveling across the country on foot in my heels!"

"Chiiiiiile," Mother drew out, stopping to bend over and laugh. "I can picture it," she teared up. "...Vera walking in her finest... trying to make a statement!"

Mug and Maxine laughed too. Apparently Mother wasn't the only one who could picture it.

"And much as I want to be like Jesus," Mother laughed, "I know I Ain't Jesus! Only Jesus can walk on water!"

"But people are buying private jets, or hiring private pilots nowadays," Shirley replied. "Stephy's husband is training for his pilot's license now, so he can fly for the Royals."

"Ooool, really Shirley," Vera cooed. "Well, let us know when he gets his pilot's license. I always wanted to get around by private jet."

Mother kept quiet, her jaws locked, swollen and tight. Sometimes Shirley got on her everlasting nerve, boasting and knowing-it-all.

Maxine kind of felt the same, but for a different reason. "That'll be the day," she scoffed. "...When everybody and their mother are flying around by private jet! They won't be satisfied until they f-up the air too."

"Ain't that the truth," Mug also scoffed. "First class not enough, now they got to have their own private jets! Wonder what's next!" And she wasn't asking.

"Hell on earth," Maxine answered.

"Well, I'll tell you one thing," Mug continued huffing. "Way up there, they're messing with my Jesus...and that's one you don't want to mess with!"

"I'm just sayin'," Maxine agreed. "This world is going to hell in a hand basket!"

"No, not the world," Mother disagreed. "Only the U.S. It's not like this everywhere. Only here where people are losing their morals and values."

"Lord Girls, what are you fussing about now," Vera teased.

"I just remember when we used to get three meals on a flight, and drinks were free," Maxine said. "And everybody on the plane was dressed up."

"Ooo yeah, remember that," Mother added.

"Yeah, but people dressed better back then anyway," Shirley slipped in, to another one of Mother's eyerolls.

"They sure didn't have fat ass nasty ba'hind stewardess like that one on that flight," Maxine scoffed, having received the brunt of vitriol from the flight attendant for insisting on calling the woman sir. "Looked like she should've been put in a cage!"

"Yeah, flight attendants don't look anything like they looked years ago," Mother agreed.

"We had more manners, and class," Maxine said. "And we certainly shaved off our moustaches and put on deodorant before we left the house."

"Ieeeeeek," Vera squealed. "Max, you a card!"

"People today just burn me up. Wanna be a woman and man. They want it all," Maxine hammered on, right up until the automatic airport doors opened, where Elaine appeared.

30.

The Elaine that met them outside the airport was nothing like the bent over, head down, black-eyed swollen lip Elaine who once upon a time lived on Gorgas Lane. This Elaine hopped out of a spanking brand-new white Escalade and ran up to the girls, back straight as an arrow, head up and a foot taller, resembling so much of a Nefertiti beauty. She greeted them with a warm hug, teeth looking like a row of chiclets. Maxine stepped back when she got to her.

"Who you?" Maxine teased. "I don't hug strangers off the street."

"Max, you haven't changed a bit," Elaine laughed, embracing her too. And it was true. Maxine hadn't changed one iota. Truthfully, none of the girls had changed much, but Maxine both acted and looked like she hadn't celebrated another birthday after turning 25.

"Well, you sure have," Maxine noted, gently fingering the long colorful scarf Elaine had wrapped around her neck, and again stepping back to check out the new Elaine's matching dashiki. "What? Are we now a Muslim woman?"

Back in the day Elaine was married to a real low-life wife-beater. Ralph used to tear her ba'hind up each and every night. From the front door to the back door, up and down the stairs. Her cries rang out from one end of the block to the other. How she stayed with a ba'hind wipe of an imbecile for so many years, gave all the girls' nightmares. There were no advocate groups rallying around these type women, and the girls, for the most part at least, didn't know how to help her.

Only Maxine and Vera dealt with her, mostly trying to convince her to leave Ralph. But she had one excuse after the other. First it was denial. He didn't mean to hurt her. Then it was the kids. They needed two parents. Then it was her fault. She didn't have domestic skills, or couldn't muster up the correct mood to smile at the asshole when he got home.

Next, she had no money. And finally, after running head on into another car, because she couldn't see out of her swollen shut eyes, an accident that resulted in the death of her only son, and the beating of her life, she took her two remaining girls and vanished.

The girls didn't know what happened to her, other than it took a head on collision to come to her senses. Back then, only her father lived in the city. He was born and raised in Philly but was a sad alcoholic. Years prior, when Elaine was a baby, her mother left the lush...leaving her precious children behind, which included Elaine, returning to her native home, Ohio, thus no family for the girls to contact.

And then, one day, several years after Elaine vanished, Vera got a call.

The chit-chat in the car was light, mostly because the girls, outside of Vera of course, were taking in the new Elaine. She talked a lot more than they'd ever known her to talk.

"I love it out here...far more than I liked living in Sacramento," she explained. "The air is lighter, and it's a lot safer."

"I don't think I could ever leave my city for good," Mug replied.

"You could if you were Elaine," Maxine muttered.

Only Mug heard her, and wasted no time responding. "Oh no, I'm not saying I would have stayed with that fool," she shot back. "I'd just be in a Philly jail," she chuckled out loud.

"Yeah, that was a difficult trial," Elaine softly replied over her shoulder. "I both regret and don't regret it."

Silence. No immediate comebacks were forthcoming. If only it wasn't for the loss of her son one of the girls would have questioned her about that remark. But her son's death was such a tragic event. His sweet little face was still engraved in their minds. Maxine used to watch him, while Elaine was in the hospital, either recovering from child-birth, or a beating.

"They say, beauty always comes out of tragedy," Elaine softly continued, her voice sounding like a rushing river. "You know...something like it takes ugly to see beauty."

"Ump," Mug muttered under her breath. Only Maxine sitting next to her, in the far rear backseat, heard her. She knew what the 'ump' meant.

Once Mug came to blows with Ralph, when he walked through her front door, inside her home, demanding that Elaine come home with him. Mug was in the kitchen at the time. She turned around and told Elaine she didn't have to leave, but he had a few seconds to get out of her house.

Ralph, who wasn't a terribly big man, turned to Mug and told her to mind her business, he'd do whatever he wanted with his wife, but if she was that bad he dared her to knock his hat off his head. He even bent over to help her out, paying no attention to the fact that she was chopping onions.

Of course she took the butcher knife and sliced his hat right off his head. If only she had swung an inch lower, instead of half the hat flying across the room, it would have been half his head.

Damn! She missed.

But then, as it would be, he grabbed Elaine and left the house, later giving her another vicious beating. It was the one reason Maxine refrained from jumping on him. So badly she wanted to, but always feared what might happen to Elaine. Mug never had that fear. What she lacked in height, she made up for in beating down anyone who crossed her line.

31

Elaine pulled up on a spacious white carport and the girls, save for Vera, thought she had stopped at a shopping mall. "I told y'all her place was gorgeous," Vera squealed.

"Not this gorgeous," Myrtle belted.

"Lord Elaine, who died and left you some spare change," Mother teased.

Shirley though, sitting beside Mother "umped," and rolled her eyes. Jealous.

"I need to find my shades," Mug in the far rear back-seat said, digging in her purse looking for her sunglasses. It was a bright sunny day, which the huge white house and plentiful white cement didn't help block the glitzy glare hitting them all right in the face.

Elaine's home was splendid. Absolutely 100% splendid. To the contrary of Mother's quip she didn't inherit the house, so-to-speak. She bought it in an auction, from money she made for her appearances in soap operas, or so she claimed.

"Really? You played in the soaps?" Mug asked, running her eyes up and down the octagon cathedral towering tall walls and Biblical hand carved columns. Everywhere her eyes landed there wasn't a thing she failed to gawk at.

"Yes, I did," Elaine replied. "Well, I was just an extra, but an extra in all the major soap operas."

"Girl, I never saw you in any soap operas," Mother said, still skeptical of how a once battered wife could achieve such grandeur.

"Because you, like the rest of us, never watched soaps," Myrtle answered for everybody. "We were busy working."

"Well Vera, did you know she played in the soaps," Mother turned and asked Vera.

"I thought I told y'all," Vera replied. "I know I told y'all how well she was doing."

Of course the girls had brushed over Vera's cooing. It was hard to discern what 'doing well' meant in Vera language, especially knowing how awful Elaine used to live.

"Didn't I show y'all pictures of her girls and the grand-babies," Vera carried on.

"Maybe it would've helped if you'd showed us pictures of this house," Mug yapped.

But for the longest, had the girls questioning Elaine's grandiose home really thought back, they would have recalled the hundreds, maybe thousands of photos she sent. Every year, after she contacted Vera… Christmas, her girl's birthdays, when her girls graduated high-school, and college…and got married… and had children… every minor and major occasion Elaine sent cards with photos. But the girls, except for Vera of course, put the cards where they put all paper products cluttering up their home. In the trash. And it wasn't that they didn't care for Elaine, or her updates. They were relieved knowing she'd gotten out of her rotten marriage and moved on. It was more like, out of sight, out of mind. They preferred getting flimsy updates from Vera, which interestingly enough, mostly went ignored as well …until now.

Elaine showed them around, taking them through a grand foyer, designed by a man they didn't know and would never remember, even if that man's name was tatted on their wallets, an object they opened each and every single day.

There were six or seven rooms on the main level; her meditating room, an exercise room, a sauna, two bathrooms, a dining room, a kitchen and then there was a sitting room and living room…which filling less than a quarter of the living room was a grand piano, a grand staircase, and the grandest goldest Christmas tree they'd ever seen standing up so high. New York's Macy's grand tree didn't compare.

"Boy, Shirley, I bet you'd like to take that one home with you," Mother rubbed in.

Usually Shirley hauled in the grandest trees, but this tree beat her little 7-foot trees she would invite everyone over to show off.

"What I want to know, is who in the devil decorated that thing," Maxine asked.

"Chile, the same people who get up there and dust off them lamps in the coliseums," Myrtle belted.

"Yeah, I guess you're right," Maxine laughed. "If Shugga can get up there and wash Comcast's windows, I guess anybody can decorate a 20-foot tree!"

Of course the girls laughed, that being everyone but Shirley, and for some reason Elaine.

"I know you're not living in here all alone," Mother scoffed.

"All by me, myself and I," Elaine smiled. "I used to believe I needed company around the clock, but found out I don't."

"Ump! Seems selfish," Shirley muttered, drowned out by Mug pouring her attention over a spread of gifts displayed beneath the tree.

"Girl, you shouldn't have," Mug cackled. "You know we can't get all this stuff home on one trip!"

Elaine threw her head back to laugh. It was an elegant move, a modest show of grace, something A-list celebs did.

"Actually, some of the gifts are for you all," she replied. "Christmas is one time of the year when I share what I've been blessed with."

32.

"How ya' like me now," Mug joked when she got behind the closed door, a room she was sharing with Mother and Shirley.

"Chile, I think I done died and am in heaven," Mother chuckled.

"Ump!" Shirley huffed. "Something ain't right," she muttered.

"The only thing that ain't right is you, if you don't enjoy these two days coming at us," Mug replied. Usually she didn't care for a whole lot of phony flair, but this was how she got when she was on vacation!

"Yeah, I'm happy for Elaine...especially after all she went through," Mother sort of agreed. "Looks like she landed on a mound of gold...for every one of those ba'hind whippins' she took."

"Well, Chester used to hit on me," Shirley muttered, slowly unfolding and refolding clothes she pulled from her suitcase. "All I ended up with was a broken heart and a daughter who's starting out making some of the same mistakes I made."

Mother let go of the chiffon curtains she had parted looking down on Elaine's elaborate figure-8 pool and spun around. "Chester used to beat you like that," she asked angered. And not angered because of Shirley's confession, but angered because she didn't remember Shirley being beat the way Elaine had been beaten.

"You didn't know that," Mug retorted. "I'm surprised you don't remember that one night, and them big 'ole medallions and chokers Chester used to wear around his neck!"

Of course Mother remembered Chester, and the whole 70's Superfly look he had going on. And she most certainly remembered that one night when Shirley's marriage had come undone.

But who among them hadn't run up on a time when their marriage turned that one dark corner? Joe wasn't always the lump on a log he was now. One night, after the worst fight in their marriage, he left, and she feared was the last she'd see of him. He hadn't hit her, and he did eventually return, but it didn't change the fact that they all experienced that one knock-down drag-down fight.

"Well, I didn't get whipped like Elaine, "Shirley quietly said. "But our marriage hit rock bottom too—"

"—But you got to leave all that where it is," Mug chastised, and she wasn't referring to Shirley staying in a broken marriage. Chester left her. Once he got out of jail, he packed his things and moved in with a white woman who lived in a raggedy one-bedroom apartment above a bar. He never looked back, not even to see his children. For years Shirley tried to get back at him, to make him wish he had never done what he'd done. She lost weight… started dressing better… took him to court and made him pay dearly. She even had a cousin chase him out of the city. For several years no one knew where Chester was, until he popped up in King of Prussia with wife number three, and three more children.

It was Shirley's heart that Mug referred to. She never got over her broken marriage. "Throwing salt at Elaine 'cause she did what you can't or won't do ain't gonna change the picture," Mug said.

Shirley didn't reply. Quietly she continued reorganizing her suitcase, unlike Mother who ventured out on the balcony for a better inspection of the pool. "Shirley is right," she said when Mug joined her. "You don't get all of this off no extra chump change."

"Oh yeah," Mug shot back. "I don't care how she got it! They better come and get me before Sunday get here because I'm enjoying this while I can!"

33

They were served a meal on the deck, for when Elaine said she lived alone, didn't mean she was in the house alone. Staff lived on the property with her. She hired a full-time chef, a landscaper, and a team of service professionals, from masseuses to housekeepers to help out during the girls' visit.

"Oh, this isn't the norm," she chuckled a laugh West coasterners pulled off with ease. "I have a friend who visits. And from time to time I still do my own cooking and laundry."

"Well, do you have to call a taxi to get from your bedroom to your laundry room," Maxine teased.

"Chile you'd have to cut me out that bedroom," Myrtle howled. "Have y'all seen her bedroom? It has everything in there!"

Elaine's bedroom was so large that it had two bathrooms…a her, and sort of like his bathroom. The bed itself was big enough that all seven of them could have slept in it, and still had room for Shugga.

"This is way too much house for me," Maxine chuckled. "I'd probably need GPS just getting from one room to the next."

"Well, I'd be worried about someone slipping in here and getting me," Mother said. "Are there deadbolts on your bedroom door," she asked Elaine.

"Girl, it's a security code on the door," Myrtle answered for Elaine. "Like I said, I'd just live in there. It has everything! Even a kitchenette!"

"So, how've you been," Elaine asked Shirley who hadn't parted her lips to so much as sip the canned Smart Water sitting in front of her.

"Just fine," she replied, wearing a thin small smile. "I not too long ago just got back from London. My son-in-law works for the Royals," she threw in, interrupted by Mother's deep sigh.

"Stephy just had triplets," Mother inserted, offering news she thought unnecessarily left on a back burner. "And didn't you say Bobby is stationed in Hawaii, commanding some military base?" she turned and asked Shirley.

Shirley flinched, just as irritated by Mother as Mother often was with her, but went on graciously filling Elaine in on the what-abouts of her children and grandchildren. She even used the spotlight on her to stab at the beef bourguignon served by waiters wearing white hats and sterling long white napkins draped over their arm.

"Oooh, Stephy took me to this one restaurant that served the best beef bourguignon I've ever tasted in my life," she said as if poking at her food wasn't speaking for her.

"Would you like something else," Elaine asked. "We also have braised rabbit—"

"—Oh no," Shirley said cutting her off with a neck snap and eye-roll. "I ate on the plane!"

"What!? When'd you eat on the plane," Myrtle blurted.

"I brought a hoagie with me," Shirley huffed. "I don't bother with that airplane food!"

Nobody said nothing, because everyone knew this was how Shirley was…marching to her own beat, something like her sister Shugga, albeit in polar opposite directions. Eventually the grandeur wore her out. The chefs, maître'd's and waiters calling them ma'dams, refilling their glasses every time they took a sip …Elaine's newfound wealth and giving back…the figure-8 pool and the 3-million dollar home…the 20-foot Christmas tree and the 1500 thread count patterned sheets…the soap operas and dozens of bathrooms…the five-car garage and the button they could press if they needed anything at all… all wore on Shirley. She excused herself to deal with the jet lag, leaving Elaine and the girls in the sitting room enjoying coffee, cognac and crème brûlée.

"Is Shirley okay," Elaine asked.

"She's fine," Maxine scoffed. "You know there's always one party pooper in every group."

Truth was, before Elaine it was Shirley who, in fact, acted just like Elaine. Every time the girls turned around, they'd hear about a thousand dollars she got for Mother's Day, or how Stephy's husband paid her mortgage so that she could stay in London for a couple of months. This would be the son-in-law who one day was everything, and the next day nothing. One time Mug parted her curtains to see a brand-new Jeep Cherokee with a big bright yellow bow wrapped around it parked in front of Shirley's house. One of her sons parted with that gift. But there were also the cousins who bought her designer purses. And people at her job gifting her trips. That's how they got to go to Bermuda, and cruise around the Mediterranean, though they had to scrape together money to go. It wasn't lost on them how more relaxed she was on those trips.

None-the-less, she didn't brag about the gifts, but played them down, something like what Elaine seemed to be doing. And true too, the girls weren't innocents. At various times they played the humble card too.

"I wished someone told me to bring my bikini," Mug teased looking through French doors facing the patio. "I could go for a dip in that pool right about now," she laughed.

"Well, I'm sure glad nobody didn't," Maxine teased too. "And I'm sure these hombre guapos are glad too," she laughed louder, as did the other girls.

"Chile, it's about 30 degrees back home," Myrtle belted, elbow propped up on a leather buttoned sofa with the rolled arms, holding a lit Virginia Slim in the air, the fumes collected by an air purifier Elaine brought out and turned on, for her sole personal use. "Nobody hardly was thinking about floating in water," she chuckled.

"You guys are still the same," Elaine noted for about the hundredth time since they arrived. She genuinely was pleased with their company.

"Chile, tigers don't change its stripes," Maxine laughed.

"All except one," Myrtle muttered, trying to hold back the laughter.

"Who," Elaine asked, not catching her drift.

"Who do you think," Mother chimed in.

"I always marveled at the way you guys took care of each other," Elaine said, ignoring the inside joke. "You all were the best thing that ever happened for me."

"Awww," Vera cooed, smiling but saying little.

"Well, I'm glad to hear that," Myrtle belted. "I always felt so bad about all that mess you had to go through, and not being able to do anything."

"Actually women in those situations are just like those in drug rehabs," Maxine added. "They have to want to take that first step themselves."

"That's just what I was telling Mother," Mug replied.

"It's hard though," Vera chimed in. "Sometimes it takes more than willpower to escape them bad situations. There are some real hateful men out here."

"I definitely know that," Elaine sighed. "I was married to one."

"But you got out and we're glad you did," Vera cooed.

"Now we got to worry about the other one," Myrtle belted, feet kicked up and crossed at the ankles, blowing Slim fumes in the direction of the purifier.

"Oh my goodness, who?" Elaine asked.

"The only one who isn't here," Mother replied.

"Shirley," Elaine gasped.

"No, the only one among us keeping more secrets than all of us combined," Myrtle teasingly huffed.

34

Funny, the reason Elaine didn't get the joke, was because she knew about both the show and Shugga, even before they did. Her and Shugga had always been in contact, though no one knew this, to include Vera, and Shugga's own sister Shirley, and not due to any conscious intent to deceive anyone.

Fact was, they never lost contact, something they kept to themselves early on, mostly to prevent her abusive ex-husband from tracking her down. The two formed a genuine friendship long before it became community knowledge her ex-husband was a wife beater. Shugga didn't always work on scaffolds washing windows. Her first job was in the hospital, back in the day when hospitals smelled like rubbing alcohol, and the environment inside so sterile that everything except the stainless-steel carts and operating tools were white. Shugga was the only other exception.

One night when Ralph was just the boyfriend, he beat her up on the subway, after a man getting off at his stop winked at her. That night the ambulance came for both her and Ralph, because riders on the train tried to stomp his heart out. Both were taken to Einstein, where Shugga who was then a LPN, first met Elaine.

From the get-go Shugga mesmerized her. It wasn't only the fact that she was one of the first black women to hold a major position in a large general hospital, but it was her bright green eyes, and the fact that she was black, and most surprising of all...she lived on Gorgas Lane!

Over the years they kept the friendship to themselves, again out of no conscious intent to deceive. It's just that while the girls teased Shugga about her expansive book knowledge, which not only included polemics on religion and medicine, what ultimately led to her being ousted from the hospital, but doctrines on every.single.thing, Elaine respected her prowess to medicate the mind, and adversity to gossip.

So a break in conversation to introduce this longstanding friendship never materialized. But had Shugga, or Elaine, told just one of the girls they were in contact way back when, it would have been like getting on CNN and telling the world. The girls were sweet, but unaware their mouths were the worst vaults for keeping secrets. That's why, and little did they know, their reality debut was anticipated to be a smashing hit.

The following evening, at dinner, a day before their departure Maxine mentioned how she couldn't wait for Shugga to return to the states "...with the rich African."

"What you gonna do," Vera teased, winking at Myrtle. "...throw them an after-party?"

"Oh, I'ma throw her an after-party alright," Maxine chuckled. "...Running off and marrying some rich African without telling nobody," she playfully scoffed.

"Chile, she probably got tired of taping them nickels and dimes to envelopes to mail her bills," Myrtle belted.
The girls fell back laughing. That being all of them except Elaine who muttered, "...rich African?"

"Oh, we're sorry," Maxine replied to Elaine's furrowed brows. "You probably haven't heard. Shugga quit her job, left the country, and married some rich African," she flatly stated.

"Interesting," Elaine quietly said. "I didn't know Cory was wealthy," she added.

"Cory?" Mug muttered, meanwhile Shirley's eyes are alert, her head moving, looking from Maxine to Elaine, to Vera and Mug.

"Wait a minute," Maxine said. "How do you know his name? Shugga has yet to call us and confirm—" and before finishing the sentence she looked over at Shirley. "—Have you talked to Shugga yet?"

"I already told y'all, I don't know nothing," Shirley said, her dowdy expression confirming what everyone knew.

She was last on Shugga's list of confidants. Not because she had a big mouth like everyone else in the room, except for Elaine…and maybe Vera, and albeit, only when it came to telling other folks business. Shugga didn't talk to her sister because they argued about every single thing. It was hard for the sisters to come to a meeting of the mind when both knew so much. The two had a rivalry going on the size of Cain and Abel.

Without missing a beat Elaine replied, "she just sent me a Christmas card."

"Oh Lord Elaine, let us see a picture of Shugga's new man Cory," Vera cooed.

Promptly Elaine got up and retrieved the card right off the mantle, within view of where the girls sat chowing down on lobster thermidor and smoked salmon pates. She opened the card and the photo slipped out. Quickly Mother scooted over closer to Vera, and Maxine hopped out of her seat and hurried around the table. She couldn't wait for the photo to be passed around. This picture she had to see right away.

Mother burst out laughing, completely drowning out Vera's soft muffled chuckle. When Maxine looked down, she burst out laughing too, hurrying off with the picture to show Myrtle.

"Oh Lord Jesus! Jesus Christ!" Myrtle shouted. "Don't tell me my girlfriend done hooked up with a Somalian!"

"He gotta be paying her. He gotta be paying her. Ain't no way," Maxine said.

"Well I'll be a monkey's uncle," Mug chuckled when she saw the picture. "Look like Shaggy and Scooby Doo!"

The girls cried laughing, wrapped around each other, sliding out of their seats, slapping the table…they rolled. Well, that being all except for Elaine and Shirley…and somewhat Vera.

35

The girls could thank their lucky stars, or count their blessings that airline stewardess wasn't on the return flight. They definitely would've been ejected, mid-flight, had that woman heard them at the back of the plane cutting up... 4.5 hours non-stop.

Because the girls had grown a little skeptical of Elaine, at times questioning her demeanor and the whole castle thing, they refrained from keeping it real in real time. Between Rod the chef who seemed offended after Mug slapped his hand, telling him she could reheat her own plate, and Elaine floating around in the Egyptian cotton kimonos passing out gifts, they tried to be on their best behavior.

Elaine bought them all jewelry...from Tiffany's...things she remembered about them. Mother got a bracelet. Vera a brooch. Myrtle a ring. Maxine earrings. Mug a nose-ring. And Shirley received a Tiffany figurine. Interestingly enough, the gifts were equitably similar. Maxine and Myrtle later, indecorously, checked. Each gift cost in the $1500 price range...an exorbitant amount of money to spend on friends who hadn't given a really good reason for why they hadn't bothered to so much as open the greeting cards she sent over the years. The entire environment just created too many distractions to fully let loose.

Not on this plane ride. At the back of a plane, elevated 35,000 miles in the sky, and no uptight stewardesses on board, was perfect for letting their hair down and mouths run.

"That was no rich African I saw on that picture," Mother started laughing.

"Chile, I saw the iron marks on his suit," Myrtle belted.

"And did you check out his feet," Mug blurted.

"Girl, you know Africans got rough feet," Myrtle said.

"But he was wearing a dern suit with them bad boys," Mug argued.

"And green," Maxine added, all of them falling out, the plane rocking from side to side each time a different girl opened her mouth and they laughed.

"Chile, his feet look liked them ostrich's feet Felipe put on the table," Mug howled.

"Aaaiaiiiieee," Vera squealed. "Y'all need to stop it right now," she howled anyway.

"I know," Mother agreed, though laughing the hardest. "First she was in the mayor's mouth, now she's on this man's feet!"

"Girl, I know one thing," Maxine cackled speaking to Mug. "You better leave African's feet alone. They got slingshots! They'll stone ya' ba'hind!"

"Yeah, and them Somalians are some cutthroats too," Myrtle belted.

"No chile, that's them Nigerians," Maxine corrected.

"Oh no," Myrtle argued. "Them Somalians are the cutthroats. The Nigerians just like to rob you."

"Whichever one is what, don't matter," Mother fussed laughing. "Neither one of 'em are rich!"

"Chile, a nickel will buy 'em a clay house, an elephant and 8 wives," Myrtle howled.

And they fell out laughing again.

"Well, I sure hope Shugga got more than a nickel on this deal," Maxine laughed, barely able to catch her breath getting the sentence out. "I made the same mistake!" she blurted.

The girls laughed so hard, though not at Maxine who they either hadn't heard, or lost in the repartee talking over each other laughing about Cory and Shugga. The only one really listening was Shirley. But if she was collecting and counting up secrets, she remained inconspicuous, laughing almost as hard as everyone else, to include a few passengers sitting nearby.

This factor really fueled the girls. They had an audience.

"Chile, wouldn't it be something if Shugga returned knocked up," Mother threw into the stewing howl of laughter, simmering the howling down to a somber minutes' worth of reflection.

"Chile please," Mug scoffed. "Shugga is 69-years old!"

"Unt un," Myrtle disagreed. "Last year a woman gave birth at 66."

"Yeah, but that woman probably had sex before," Mug contended.

And zip. They all stopped jabbering for a second before howling so loud they drowned out the drumming hum of the engines, bringing a handful of flight attendants to the rear of the plane.

"Oh sugar, we're alright," Maxine told one attendant, as Vera waved a Franklin at another. She wanted to buy drinks for her friends, which her request was almost denied, with the lot of them acting like they'd already had one too many.

But Mug stepped in, because that was what friends did for each other. "Look, our best friend, who is 69-years old and just might be a virgin, just married an African ...out of the blue... with some bad feet...who we never met," she began her plea in earnest. "Now, I'm speaking about the man...not the feet," she continued, to which even the flight attendants couldn't help but chuckle.

"Tell the truth," she continued to bait amid sustained laughter. "Wouldn't you want a drink if you were in our seats?"

"Y'all a mess," Shirley chuckled, trying to keep a straight face, except her shoulders vibrated so hard, it gave her away. "Shugga, and that African, are gonna hang all of y'all when they get back here."

"No, Shugga gonna have to tell me something when she get back here," Maxine said.

"Oh, don't worry, she will," Mug laughed. "Won't no duct tape in the world be enough to stop her," she cackled.

"Chile, if you duct taped her mouth, them eyes would get to talking," Maxine muttered.

The girls were back in stitches, recalling times when Shugga ran her mouth, against better judgement...the premier memory being the time she got to arguing with a voter-volunteer at a polling place about being discriminated against.

She pointed in the man's face, calling him the ku klux klan, demanding to speak to his boss, with her huge pocketbook covering everything on the desk, to include the man's hands. Her ancestors had fought, tooth and nail, through poll taxes, grandfathered-in clauses, police dogs, Birmingham jails, lynchings…she even brought Emmett Till into the fold, for her right to vote. She wasn't able to be moved, until another volunteer intervened, asking if she was mentally sound. Shugga went nuts, absolutely ballistic, acting further the fool. The volunteers had swapped shifts and a million people had voted before she was finally pulled off the proverbial mountain top…the one Dr. Martin Luther King Jr. spoke about, and showed the 'mental disabled' box she, herself, accidentally checked on the voter registration form.

"Oh Lord, I got to go to the bathroom," Myrtle belted out loud, flight attendants having scurried off to get the drinks and attend to other business, leaving her to pull herself up out the seat all on her own. She used the back of the seat in front of her, accidentally catching a passenger's hair in the process.

"I'm sorry Chile," she apologized, turning to mutter out the corner of her mouth at the girls. "Thank Jesus I didn't pull the whole seat down," starting the girls back up again.

"Alright now, be nice," Vera chuckled, playing referee. "We almost got thrown off the other bus mid-flight," she teased. "I'm not trying to get ejected before I get my drink!"

"Aww, they'll be alright," Mother muttered. "If we got through it, they'll get through it."

"Ooo Chile, tell me about it," Mug scoffed. "But won't God do it," she said, eyes closed holding up a prayer fist.

"Yes Lord," Maxine and Vera hummed, grateful for an animus that could have been as opposite as Satan was to an angel.

"Chile Mama used to burn us up," Mug continued in prayer mode, eyes still closed and shaking her head, "knowing good and well how hard it was to feed the mouths she had, yet she'd leave for work, and all be damn return home with another mouth to feed!"

"Ooo! Ain't that the truth," Maxine huffed, shaking her head too. "I'm surprised I'm not celibate!"

"Yeah, I'm surprised I ever had children too," Mother chuckled. "I still don't know how Joe got me pregnant since I don't ever remember him touching me!"

The girls howled. Maxine laughing the hardest. "Wait a minute now Mother. Was it that bad?"

"It was worse," Mother continued. "I still remember him climbing on me with his shoes on."

And they laughed harder.

"Lord have mercy Mother," Vera chuckled. "With his shoes on," she cooed.

"Ooo, I heard y'all all the way in the latrine, over the dern engines," Myrtle chuckled. "Can't take y'all nowhere," she teased, carefully easing into her seat.

"Well, if people would stop running off to marry rich Africans, at 69-years old, we wouldn't be laughing," Mother cackled.

"Wait a minute now, but who said Cory was rich," Vera asked.

The back of the plane fell silent again. The girls stopped teasing and laughing to think back.

"Mother told me," Mug finally said.

"Unt un," Mother protested. "You told me," she said putting the blame on Mug.

"No I didn't. You called me and—"

"—No Mug, remember? The detectives were the ones that came to your house."

"Oh yeah, that's right," Mug remembered. "It was the detectives that started this mess!"

"Lord have mercy, them producers are going to catch hell with y'all!"

"You mean us," Mother corrected.

"No, I mean y'all," Myrtle scoffed. "I ain't fooling around with y'all on national TV!"

36

Despite only spending two days away, and in lieu of grander itineraries they had experienced before, and besides the scene caused after Maxine's daughter-in-law didn't pick her up from the airport, they, in unison, returned home calling this one of the best vacations they'd taken in years.

"Oh my gosh, we laughed so hard," Mother shared with co-workers gathered around her desk. She worked in customer service for a bank, answering calls to settle billing issues, address changes and the likes. It was perfect work for a boomer like her. Not too taxing on the mind or body. The work was suited perfectly for AARP centurions like Mother, already collecting social security.

For three hours, three times a week, she entertained her co-workers with stories about her family and friends. This time she scooped up highlights of her trip to Arizona, and by the mouthful fed them to those huddled around her desk. She bragged about Elaine's castle...the servants...the food... the lavish gifts, showing off her Tiffany bracelet in case someone needed proof. And despite the big boss being in the huddle too, she told them how she didn't want to leave.

Well, Patty was there to collect Mother's log sheet for the day. And Jordana was on her way home. Charmaine, sitting a cubicle away, had only pushed her seat back, so she really couldn't be counted, like Lakesha Watkins, on her way to the bathroom.

"Ms. Catherine, who's business you spreadin' now," Lakesha asked, in that eye-cutting city attitude.

Just so happened, Mother was in the middle of sharing Elaine's awful background. This was an integral part of the story, given the big boss was asking, curious about her friend's wealth and how she had come upon it.

Mother swung her chair around, to address Lakesha directly. "I sure as heck am not talking about you and Fred," she replied. "And by the way, his wife just pulled up in the parking lot, so you should have a whole 15 extra minutes on your call log today."

Patty let her head drop and shook it. Jordana chuckled, shaking her head too and turned on her heels, headed for the exit. Charmaine, humored none, made a bee-line, straight for the bathroom. And Mr. Elliot Rossi, he laughed, and walked away too.

Had Mother been just a decade younger, and perhaps working a couple of miles East of where she sat, and talking to her co-workers like this, she in high likelihood would have been among the city's high fatality rate.

"Ms. Catherine, aren't you worried about getting someone in trouble," Patty asked after the group dispersed.

"Heck no!" Mother replied. "Why should I be worried? I'm not messing around with someone else's husband!"

"No, I'm talking about your friend in Arizona. Elaine." Mother thought for a second. She couldn't figure out what she said so wrong.

"Don't you know Mr. Rossi was an IRS auditor?"

Mother thought about this remark for a second too. Sometimes she was accused of being a little too trusting and naïve, like it wasn't lost on her that productive people talked about ideas, and small minds talked about...well, nothing. But, so what? What was the big deal about getting carried away in the moment? Deep in her heart she really meant no harm. And still, she couldn't figure out what she said so wrong.

"Chile, our girlfriend used to get her tail whipped everyday...horrible beatings," she said squeezing her eyes shut and shaking her head to shut out the memory. "So, if Elliot wants to audit someone, he should audit that!"

"Well, you should be careful. You made it sound like even you are suspicious of where your friend got the money," Patty replied.

"And I still am," Mother shot back. "But even if she got it from sleeping on a lot of casting couches, the ones who need to be investigated about where all that money came from, are the ones giving it away! You know…like all his rich friends!"

Patty laughed, almost as hard as they laughed during the 4.5-hour plane ride. "Only you Ms. Catherine," she chuckled wiping tears from her eyes. "I sure would like to meet your friends one day. Y'all sound like a lot of fun."

"Aww, Girl, we are, and you can," Mother replied. "You can catch us on Real Women, Channel 101. It airs Christmas Eve, but they're taping us this weekend."

37

Maxine was in Shoppers, where she worked a few days a week, handling financials. She'd worked retail since high-school, over half a century wearing every hat but the owner's hat. And now, two decades after getting her AARP card, she was finally promoted to the front office, where she was scheduled on the day the big boss Mark Cousins, a young kid dressed in a white shirt and Christmas necktie, graced the store with a visit.

Just so happened Mark made this visit a day after she and the girls returned from Arizona. Normally she'd be locked in the shoebox of an office, sitting room for one only, paper-clipping receipts and sending reports, and praying an issue didn't crop up, that she would have to leave the shoebox to handle. Decades ago, when she was in her teens, she dreamed about reaching this plateau, but not now. Now she hid in the bunker, fearing someone she knew might come in and recognize her, in her supposed glory years, still working on the plantation.

As it would be, when the big boss paid the store a visit, the store authority Nancy, a forty-year old Miss Sally who loved beating her chest and corralling in attention, ordered everyone in to work, albeit without telling anyone the big boss was coming in, otherwise this incident would've never occurred. Maxine was too seasoned and too retired from the Miss Sally treatment to put up with being bossed around in front of a big boss kid.

But unaware of the big boss visit Maxine arrived at work to find Nancy in the store dressed in a navy Christmas blazer, just barking up a storm for visibility. On this day, pinned to the jacket was a brooch to support the troops, America, the LGBT community, cancer survivors, the ozone...and oh, she had room for her employee badge.

Tom was also in the store, which these two, Nancy and Tom, never worked together. But Tom, the official charge, had no choice, odd as that would seem. He and Nancy were like hot and cold, fire and ice. Maxine though, liked the 70-year old transplant. He was an easygoing man, native of Altoona, who only cared about resolving issues safely, quickly and equitably, and in that exact order. He didn't want no drama, the best man on staff far as Maxine was concerned. She almost could marry a man with those values, except Tom was white. She couldn't picture a white man climbing on top of her in the middle of the night. Wasn't no telling how she might react. She might open her eyes and resurrect an ancestor; Tubman, or Miss Pittman, or Sula, or Tar Baby, or any one of them not so much resting in peace. Nope. Couldn't do it, though otherwise she and Tom worked together well.

Danielle, or Dani as Nancy called the twenty-some-thing year old child, was in the store as well. The girl had zero class, growing up in Langhorne where the store was located, but acting like she'd been abandoned as a baby and left on a hill in West Virginia. She had a nerve to be intolerant of what she viewed as stupidity; one of her favorite limericks being 'she wasn't doing stupid that day.'

Soon as Maxine stepped in the door and saw all of them in there; Nancy in the booth, Dani at the front desk beneath the booth, and Tom helping one of the stockers in an aisle, she wanted to turn around and go home. Her weekend getaway had been so awesome that she didn't want to ruin it this way.

Nancy spotted her walking in and right away punched the intercom. "Maxine, come to the service desk. Maxine, come to the service desk."

Ugh! But that woman had to have good instincts. She had to have zeroed in on Maxine's mood, begging to show the big boss what she was really made of.

Maxine heard her the first time, though annoyed, and for kicks, walked over to produce and picked over bags of cran-berries, her version of trying to go Zen.

"Maxine, report to the service desk. Maxine, report to the service desk. Maxine, report to the service desk. Maxine, report to the service desk. Maxine, report to the service desk..." over and over Nancy repeated this phrase.

Now, the first thing employees did when arriving for work was clock in, which the time clock was fixed to the front office booth where Nancy hovered above. She also knew good and well, Maxine's shift started at 9am. Not 8:55, or 8:58, or 8:59 even, but 9 on-the-dot a.m.! Technically Maxine could clock in at 9:00 and 59 seconds and still be on time, which in this case she was early by 73 seconds.

Cashiers, baggers, shoppers, stockers, Tom, everyone in the store...even babies opening their eyes for the first time, along with Mark Cousins of course, all looked over to the echo emanating from the service booth.

Maxine eventually lolly-gagged over to the time clock, as if she was the only one who hadn't heard or seen Nancy, and started to clock in, but was stopped by the raging bull. Nancy burst out of the bunker screaming. "Didn't you hear me page you!? I saw you look right at me! You heard me page you. I know it! I know it! We looked right at each other!"

Her ragged voice sounded like it was being stretched apart. Her teeth looked like razors and her eyes like fresh fire. They turned colors, from yellow to orange to brick red and burnt black, with flashes of white mixed in. Normally she was quite pale, but on this morning her complexion mirrored that of a pumpkin.

Maxine looked at her anyway, fearing the bull none. She had just experienced one of the best vacations in her life. The devil himself couldn't pull her out of the cloud her mood chilled in.

To Nancy's fortune Mark Cousins appeared, and waved her back into the booth. He looked around and waved everyone else away too. During the waving Dani, the up and coming little boss, approached Maxine. "Umm you," she said pointing a tiny pale finger at Maxine's nose. "I need you in produce!"

It didn't matter that Tom was there. Or the big boss kid Mark. Or a dozen or so others. Maxine would have replied the same had it been just her and Dani.

"I don't take orders from you," she said, and turned and walked away. Shucks, that child's name was not on any of her checks, and never had been.

Mark slipped on a coat and ran after Maxine. They'd never really talked before. He was much too above for either of them to bother.

"Hey, Max," he called out, catching up with her.

He surprised her, calling out to her in that over familiar way. "What's going on?" he asked. "How about we sit in the car and chat," he said, which surprised her more. In another five minutes, after she got the other leg in the car, she would've been off, never knowing this big boss cared enough to chase after her.

"I didn't even clock in and already I'm exhausted," she sighed.

"You know, 90% of our troubles are not the event, but how we respond to it," he replied.

Nice sentiment, one she heard before, but she couldn't take this kind of philosophy from a kid. He was the big boss of the store, not wisdom.

And then the first tear fell. And then another. And another. Next thing she knew, she was sprouting tears like a hydrant. Forget being at work, or in the presence of her kid big boss, she had never! never in her life cried as hard.

"Hey... What's wrong," Mark asked, lightly massaging her shoulder.

Ashamed, for the last thing she imagined was crying in front of a kid boss, she briefly explained the trip to Arizona, the big house, and talking out loud without thinking about what she was saying, she insinuated Elaine was a thief.

"So, you think your friend stole a big 'ole visible house?" he chuckled.

"No, of course I'm not saying that," Maxine replied. "Though she could be squatting or something," she chuckled, before getting at what she meant.

"We were only there a weekend. But coming from nothing to—" —and she let her thoughts die there. Why was she even talking about this stuff? Actually, exactly what was she talking about? She had to think for a second.

"You know, I've seen some crazy stuff in my 71 years," she sighed. "I still remember a guy who came in the store and unloaded all of his fake twenties on us?"

"Yeah, but that was a low-end ring," Mark said. "They barely got away with a hundred bucks, and had to split it three ways," he chuckled.

"I don't know what I'm feeling right now," she admitted. "Maybe I'm just tired. It's hard to have tasted Alice's Wonderland, and then come back to this!"

"Well, if you want more of my two cents," he chuckled. "I hope you don't quit. It's cool if you want to take off today, but we really need you."

"Un hun," she chuckled. "But now, does any of this come with more dollars and—"

"—Actually, it does," Mark replied cutting her off. "I'm in a holiday spirit. I came to the store to give out bonuses, but I think I want to promote you instead."

Maxine gasped, bringing a hand to her chest. "But I—"

"—You don't have to give me an answer right away," he said, again cutting her off. "I don't like what I saw. I come from a family where I was taught to respect my elders, no matter what their station in life."

"Yeah, but I—"

"—I just want you to think about if you would like to handle some of our backend work, stuff you can do from home," he explained.

"Oh I see," Maxine wryly chuckled. "You're trying to get me out of sight."

"That's not it at all," he replied, face straight as a ruler. "If you want to stay at this store, you can. If you want to come in when you want…you know… to get out of the house…that's fine too," he shrugged. "Like I said, I'm in a holiday mood. I'm letting you call the shots. It's your decision, but," he said, interrupting her thoughts, "you don't have to make a decision right away."

A line was wrapped around the building when Mug arrived at work. She looked at her watch. It was a little after 11:30am. She was a few hours late.

So fire her. At her age, after decades slugging through ten feet of snow, or fighting hurricanes raining cats and dogs, or sweating it out under boiling 300-degree heat, she'd get there when she got there.

Telling the real truth, she only kept working to get out of the house, and maybe to avoid killing Oscar. Long ago she'd done the math on getting rid of debt. Going by interest rates creditors charged her, added to her spending, minus minimum payments she was making, she'd be debt free in 32- 33 years max. Yep, she laughed every time she thought about it.

She was in that mindset when she entered the social services building, packed wall to wall, with desperation, a half century old story. The cast of characters only changed when one died, bequeathing its destitution for the next of kin to inherit.

"Lori needs to speak to you," Shina, a young chunky woman who reminded Mug a lot of Miss Piggy, said.

Woo, just looking at that child really irked Mug. Why O why young girls failed to see what they really looked like? Them 26 to 46 straight inch front laced weaves and wigs took her back to minstrels shows where white people actually used this look to mock them and humor themselves.

So Mug smiled, to avoid thinking about everything else the woman reminded her of. If the other brown clown wanted to speak to her, then the other brown clown was going to have to have to come out of her little brown foxhole and do her own dirty work.

A few minutes later, just about to open her window, Lori appeared at her side. "Umm, Julia, I need to speak with you in my office right now," she said with her back to people packed wall to wall and wrapped around the building.

"Are you sure," Mug asked, looking from her to the mob glaring their way.

Had Lori bothered to turn around she would've noticed, out of eight windows, only one was opened. Anyone would want to know why two whole abled bodies were standing in front of so many unopened windows, helping no one, when the room was packed with so much helplessness.

But Lori neither turned around nor cared. "I'm sure," replied the graduate of one of the sacrilegious Mary colleges. "Get your things and come with me," she ordered, about to turn on her heels and head to her foxhole.

"Umm Lori," Mug called after her, using her outside voice, as if seeking the attention of a neighbor down the street.

The child spun around, her expression a cross between hate and nauseated.

"If I get my things," Mug said at the street level loud, "I am walking out that door, catching the trolley, and going home. Do.You.Hear.Me?"

The child hesitated, a split second her button eyes darting around as if looking for voices in the air. Looked like she was about to say never mind, except that moment was swallowed by another Miss Piggy throwing a child, purse, elbow and attitude on the counter.

"One of y'all better open this got-damn window," the woman huffed, swiping at a strand of Miss Piggy hair tangled on one of her lashes.

Mug looked at the woman, as did Lori, both staring for separate reasons. One asking, the other demanding, and all three, from three distinct socio-economic classes, wanting the same thing. Respect.

And this was the crux of Mug's issue working for social services. Every single person in the building, from Lori running the office, to her and Shina working a notch above minimum wage, to the armed guards working at minimum wage, and the countless souls crammed in the building, if they pooled every last cent to their name, it just might equal the gross salary the average CEO made in an hour.

It was a disgrace all those people were in there begging for a few coins, and a sacrilegious act to take charge of overseeing such a disgrace.

Lori looked at the woman huffing as she typed in her phone, and told her she was going to have to take a seat, until someone was available to help her.

"Do you see one fuckin' seat available in here," the woman barked, pouting as the person she called answered. "I'm gonna be late," she told whoever answered her call. "It's wall to wall people in here," she pouted, swiping at the hair and wiping away a tear.

Mug was just about to beg Lori to let her open a window, which was the other thing that bothered her, besides the fact that 95% of the people waiting for help were going to be turned away for lack of a superficial document their case couldn't be processed without anyway. Almost everyone who came through the system, the workers knew by first name. "Chile Twiggy came in today," and "they cut Nookie off for letting Gus back in," yet when Twiggy or Nookie appeared at the window it would be, "name? Address? When's the last time you worked?" The workers treated the cases like transients who mysteriously appeared in the city. It was sickening. Text book dysfunction.

Seriously! The country had world class technology to send men to the moon, and hunt down Sadam and Osama, but couldn't build a system that would limit the need for this type dysfunction.

But just as Mug was about to beg Lori to let her open a window ticket #643 jumped on a counter shouting, "I will light this MF up if somebody don't open up more of dees' windows!"

Darnell, a known city cowboy, couldn't have expressed better what Mug wanted to scream. Both guards drew their revolvers and struck the pose, but froze. The mob seeing this went wild, yelling and screaming and throwing what they could lift at the bullet proof glass.

Mug looked at Lori, her head tilted at an angle asking, 'are you going to open this window, or do you want me to do it?' But Lori stayed planted in place, her lips glued together like her

her feet were stuck to the floor.

The riot was in full swing when Mug left the protection of the cage to address the mob. Funny, but the guards hadn't budged either. They were still crouched and pointing the guns, looking much like statutes in a war museum. Interesting. They knew how to drag out Twiggy and Nookie crying for cash aid to buy food for their innocent babies wrapped around their legs, but couldn't do a thing to stop a riot, except call for assistance, a step already taken care of by those hiding behind the bullet proof glass.

It was a comical spectacle seeing Mug with her little short self moving with purpose, though coolly, beneath flying objects and insults bouncing off her, and the glass. It looked like a baby seal waddling through Armageddon.

"Boy, get your behind off that counter," Mug ordered. The mob seeing this piped down almost instantly.

"Come with me. I'm going to deal with your case in the back," she said.

Darnell hopped off the counter, put the weapon away, and sheepishly grinned. "Aww, Miss Davies, Where you from?"

"North Philly," she replied. "But boy, when we get back here you better talk fast 'cause you know the police are already on the way!"

"Aww...this gun ain't real," he chuckled, be-bopping on her heels. "I picked it up from Duck Duck Goose."

Barely listening and hardly concerned Mug punched the security code on the keypad and led Darnell into the sacred area where it suddenly looked like an apocalypse had hit and everyone vanished.

"Child, that gun don't scare me...even if it did have bullets in it!" Mug meant this too. Having spent summers in the south visiting extended family, the first thing her relatives taught them was how to drive, and how to shoot. Darnell had never been off the block, let alone out of the city. If he hit anything, it would've been by mere coincidence.

"Now what you come in here for," Mug asked the child. Last week he claimed he lost his cash card. The week before that he brought in a police report to prove he had been robbed, to back up his claim for emergency assistance he requested the the week before that.

"I just came in here to see if y'all had donuts or something in here," he replied. This was something Mug occasionally supplied on her own dime. Donuts, cookies, pretzels, bite size chocolates... she would bring in and put on the information desk... if she had the time and money.

"You know Miss Davies, I don't care if I get locked up again," Darnell said sitting down and calmly folding his hands. "It's not like I have anywhere to go. This is it for me. In fact, I'd rather be locked up."

Mug wanted to take that child and wrap him in her arms, but had a job to do. One of the guards appeared, gun back in the holster but standing off to the side fingering the cuffs. She shook her head at him, in effect waving him away and turned back to Darnell.

"No, this isn't it for you," she said. "God put every one of us on earth for a reason. And baby, if you don't do another productive thing in your life, you have fulfilled His reason today. And you better believe that!"

39

"Lord, Vera! I don't know about this reality show," Myrtle belted into the phone, before any greeting, with the pillows of smoke stacks billowing around her head. "I was speaking with Sandy and it sounds like they're going to try and make fools out of us."
"Yeah, Barry kind of hinted that to me this morning," Vera agreed. "He thinks it might be a little too much visibility... for the wrong reasons..."

"Besides, I read that contract and wasn't too happy about that clause 14! That paragraph went on for far too long talking about outside parties and what they could do about the content that comes out of the interviews,"

Myrtle fussed.

"Oh, I read that," Vera replied. "But that's there to limit the network's liability if any outright crimes are discussed."

"I know exactly what it means!" Myrtle shouted. Vera wasn't the only one steeped in education. Myrtle too had been a part of the education system in Philadelphia.

Almost half a century she taught public school. She had retired, but a decade prior, for 45 years straight, save for a few pregnancies, recooping after delivering babies, she taught math at the grade school level, before substituting while in retirement. She as well served on a number of education boards. Like Vera, she was well known...and respected in the education circuit. Principals had her number on speed dial, calling her person- ally to help out in schools. And children she taught, now with grandchildren in school, still remembered her, running up to her on the street, hugging and kissing and thanking her for inspiring them. One time she jacked a child up, who ran home complaining to the mother. The mother came huffing and puffing up to school, ready to fight, until she realized the teacher was Mrs. Williams, who taught 5th grade at Emlen when she was in school!

The mother turned right around and whipped the child's butt on the spot. "That's Mrs. Williams! I know she don't lie!" she yelled while chastising the child. "Mrs. Williams won't ever jack up a child unless that child did something wrong!"

"Yeah, I think I'm with you," Vera sighed. "I might have to slip out of town. I got enough on my plate."

"I know I do," Myrtle said. "I hardly have time for a whole lot of foolishness."

"...But do you really think one of the girls has done anything that bad?"

"Chile, it ain't no telling," Myrtle sighed. "Sandy said she heard something on the radio about a surprise. But I couldn't make heads or tails out of what Sandy was talking about. That woman is crazy as a Betsy bed bug herself. She could've been talking about one of the ex's making an appearance, as well as one of us getting an award!"

Vera chuckled. "Lord Mertie, if one of them fools of mines shows up, it'll be the end of KYL!"

"Well mines is dead," Myrtle chuckled. "So, if that fool rises up, I'll know KYL is already dead!"

"Hahaha," Vera squealed laughing. "Lord Mertie, I hope they know what they're playing with."

"Chile, that's the bad thing about stupid," Myrtle scoffed. "Stupid don't know stupid."

Vera squealed laughing again. "Well, don't let me find out one of them weasels is trying to pimp somebody out."

"Oh no, not you, the original pimp," Myrtle belted chuckling. "I still can't believe Leon let you have 49% of his company!"

"Well, it was either that or spend 49% of his life behind bars," Vera chuckled. "I guess he's one of the few who chooses life over property."

"Ump," Myrtle hummed, her mind a million miles off. "Let me ask you something," she said without pausing to wait for an answer. "Have you ever seen one of these shows?"

"Haven't seen a one," Vera replied. "You know I don't watch the low budgets," she chuckled. "If it's not a historical documentary, something that can be used in the curriculum... I don't bother."

"Well Sandy said the programs puts on a lot of debut artist," Myrtle hesitantly added, as if she was thinking about changing her mind.

"Hmmm, maybe," Vera sighed. "It's just not worth my time. I already have enough on my plate."

"I know I do," Myrtle belted. "I gotta get ready for my Chapter's Christmas party next weekend."

"Me too," Vera shrieked. "I got two to go to... on the same night!"

"Chile...only you," Myrtle chuckled. "Only you..."

40

Although Myrtle and Vera were getting scoops from their networks, and based on what they were hearing were hesitant about embracing the impending interview, at this point two days away, local radio stations were turning up the dial. One mid-day jock leaked there indeed was going to be a surprise occurring on Real Women Talk. It wasn't spelled out exactly what the surprise was going to be, but sounded dicey, what got the leak circulating. Up and down Gorgas Lane neighbors were talking, creating more and more excitement in the community, and concocting more and more anxiety among the girls.

"Looks like it's just going to be me and Mug at that interview," Mother chuckled. Shucks, she didn't have as much going on as the other girls, and she loved being on the go.

"Haha," Shirley laughed. "Yeah, Mug called me last night talking about she didn't care if the program Aired on a Tuesday at four in the morning and only three people were watching, she was telling it like it was!"

"Yeah well, Vera called me last night and said Frank's mother was sick."

"Frank's mother," Shirley said snapping her head back looking alarmed. "Frank's mother been dead a hundred years! She died before he did!"

"Well, somebody in Frank's family is sick," Mother replied. "And I agree with you. I don't know why she would be fooling around with anyone in his family anyway."

"I know he had an aunt who had a stroke and for a while lived with him and his new wife," Shirley recalled. "But they put her old bitter butt in a nursing home before he ran off with Vera's money. That woman was mean as a rattlesnake. And she hated Vera's guts. Why Vera would care about her I can't imagine."

"Yeah well, Vera isn't the only one who suddenly can't make it," Mother said. "Maxine changed her mind too, and I think so did Myrtle."

"Girl, where you going," Shirley abruptly asked. They were headed to one of the church elder's homes, Brother John, for Bible Study. He lived in North Philly, an area they didn't venture to often.

"I always take 76 to get to Ridge," Mother replied. "You know I hate driving through the niggas' neighborhoods."

"But it's a straight shot up Broad," Shirley contended, looking around as if Mother had taken a short cut through woods.

"Girl, hold onto your horses, I've got this," Mother chuckled. "I don't feel like sliding down Broad Street and getting in a gun fight over running into one of these niggas' beat up double-parked Avalons!"

"Yeah, but this way is going to take us out of the way," Shirley fussed, checking her watch. "I don't want to be in North Philly after 10pm. You know how long-winded Brother John can get."

"And don't worry, we won't," Mother chuckled. "I'll cut him off in a minute!"

Mother shot down the expressway, in her smooth riding Cadillac, zipping around every single vehicle on the road, sunk down beneath the steering wheel, eyes barely over the dashboard, and hauled tail up Ridge Avenue and over Diamond Street. Her tires humped pot holes like marshmallows, narrowly missing dozens of distractions that could cold-blooded end a middle of the day joyride.

"Well, I guess that was a short cut," Shirley muttered as they pulled up in front of Brother John's neat little row home stuffed between anarchy on one side, and abandonment on the other.

"Chile, me and Jenny don't play," Mother laughed, collecting her Bible and purse and climbing out of the car. Jenny was the pet name she gave her car.

Shirley muttered under her breath and also collected her Bible and purse and hobbled out of the car.

Brother John met them at the door before they rang the bell. He was another empty-nester, at 70-plus years of age living with his wife Milly and cocker spaniel Mitsy.

"Sisters, we're all here. We were waiting on you," he greeted them at the door, dressed in plaid church slacks, a dress shirt opened at the collar and suspenders.

Inside was Sister Joan and brothers James and Nathan, and of course Milly, with Mitsy sitting in her lap. Mother and Shirley sat in the empty chairs waiting for them and picked up from where they left off at the prior class... talking about how they shouldn't open their doors to Jehovah's Witnesses, or socialize with people who didn't act Christian-like.

"The other day I went outside and found alcohol bottles in my trash can, piled this high," Brother John said at one point, demonstrating by raising his arm and thus hand over his head. "I know good and well those bottles didn't come out this house," he assured the group. "So, you know what I did," and he waited for the group to nod, in- sinuating he continue with the story. "I took those bottles out of my trash and put every one of them on top of the trash barrel next door...exactly where I knew they came from."

"Yes Lord, devil get back," Sister Joan chanted, waving a hand above her head.

"But Brother John, with all due respect, what does it matter who's trash is whose?" Mother asked. "Trash is trash!"

"Oh but Sister Catherine, it does matter," Brother John replied. "Christians have reputations to maintain. I don't want my neighbors thinking we drink that stuff!"

"Oh my goodness," Mother almost yawned. "Who but the devil is casting stones? Isn't it a sin to judge!?"

Mother didn't have to spell out her thoughts. Several Sundays back, a guest pastor invited to speak at their church, got up on the pulpit and in addition to many accusations, he accused Brother John of stealing from the church. At the end of the sermon their home pastor had to clean up the accusations. Of course Brother John was no real thief. He would never do such an awful thing on purpose. But he did have trouble with math. Couldn't count worth a lick, making countless mistakes on the building fund budget he oversaw. Brother John looked so pitiable standing on the altar facing a congregation judging him for a sin he did not intentionally commit. Pastor Elkins tried to redeem his reputation, apologizing to the congregation for the guest pastor's untimely sermon, but no words could put aside the charge.

Mother, Shirley and Mug laughed their behinds off that Sunday. Elkins could apologize for Brother John til' the cows came home, but the fact remained, there was a discrepancy with the building fund, and Brother John, nice or not, was behind it. The girls laughed, perhaps he was an innocent thief?

"Listen," Sister Milly interjected, "what's this I hear about you putting your business on TV?"

The statement stopped Mother. She was about to go on a tangent about the business of having to be phony so that outsiders believed Christians had no human flaws. Mother always contended it wasn't what being a good Christian should mean, why she in particular was encouraged to join Bible Study.

"That's right," Mother replied, swinging around to snatch Milly up with one of her hateful looks. "I absolutely want to be a part of the conversation that lets young women know what motherhood and being a woman in our time was like!"

"And how much money are they paying you to sell your soul to the devil," Milly retorted.

"I'm not getting a damn—ooops," Mother said covering her mouth before continuing. "I'm not getting one red cent," she politely lied. "I'm doing this from my heart."

"Well Sister, let's hope you direct those tuning in, to our Bible Study," Brother James said.

Mother looked over at Brother James, sounding like a halfway recovered lush, and looking just like one, with his long wet bottom lip and bloodshot eyes. She started to speak, except Shirley kicked her shin.

"Let's wrap this up," Brother John said. "Let's bow our heads and pray."

41

Maxine had turned the corner, and was about to zip up the street, park and call it a day when she hit the brakes seeing Mug walking. Tapping the horn she rolled the window down. "Woman! Get in," she yelled from the car.

Mug waved her off as best she could. She had her purse strapped across her torso, something like Rambo, and a shopping bag in each hand.

So Maxine laid on the horn.

"Girl, I only had a block to go," Mug said after shoving shopping bags in the back seat of Maxine's car and hopping in.

"Deb oughta' be ashamed of herself, with her big fat ass laying up in the house, having her mother out here catching busses in this cold."

"Chile, I don't want her picking me up in that nasty ba'hind car," Mug scoffed. "Besides, I'd rather her be home with them kids. Can't wait until they move out. Them kids are tearing up my house!"

"And what are you doing out shopping? You should've call me. I would've taken you," Maxine said, double parking in front of Mug's house.

"Chile, you know how it is when you get money and it's hot in your hand," she laughed.

"Where you get money? Lend me some," she joked.

"You didn't get your check?"

"What check?"

"Our advance. For this weekend," Mug replied. "Chile, I found the cutest shoes."

Suddenly a car pulled up behind them and the driver laid on the horn. Maxine checked the rearview mirror and saw it was Myrtle. She rolled down her window and yelled out. "Get off that horn woman. You don't have nowhere to be," she teased.

With Myrtle on Maxine's bumper Mug grabbed her bags from the backseat and went inside, leaving Maxine to continue up the street a few houses, park and hop out the car.

"Where you coming from," Maxine teased, hanging over Myrtle's car, the driver's side.

"Chile, I was at my Chapter meeting," Myrtle replied. "Now I've got to go in here and figure out how to tell one of the girls we're not going to be able to host her book-signing."

"Book-signing," Maxine said snapping her neck back.

"Yeah Chile, one of the girls in my Chapter wrote a book…and Girl, the book is a mess!"

Maxine stepped back, thinking Myrtle needed room to finish parking. But Myrtle hustled out of her car and slammed the door. "So I hear you decided not to go either," Myrtle chuckled, ignoring Maxine standing there smirking at the awful parking attempt.

In all the years she'd known Myrtle, and all the years Myrtle had been driving, the woman couldn't park, or drive a lick. One time Maxine got in the car with her and watched her ram two cars just getting out of a parking space, what explained the dings on the front and back of her brand new red SUV. Now her car was parked about 6 feet from the curb, practically sitting in the middle of the street.

"Woman, you should've went on and left your car on Broad Street," Maxine teased, shaking her head.

"What?" Myrtle asked, looking from Maxine to the so obviously crooked parking job she'd done.

"Chile, somebody is going to come through here and carry that car with them," Maxine chuckled.

"Aww…it'll be okay," Myrtle huffed, waving off the thought and going back to her original preoccupation. "So I heard you aren't going to the show this weekend?"

Maxine was slow to respond. "I don't know what I'm doing. I'm still thinking about it," she hesitantly replied.

"Oh Lord!" Myrtle suddenly hollered, with the foresight to see disaster plowing up the street.

"Damn," she hissed, as a car traveling in excess of the 15 miles per hour residential speed limit, shot by doing about 70 miles per hour, taking her side-view mirror on its journey.

"Toldja'" Maxine snickered. "But that was some damn good driving. I hope the next one that come up the street have the same skills."

"Aww…it's okay," Myrtle huffed, waving off the event. "I probably have a mirror I can tape to the car," she laughed. "You know, do like the niggas do," she laughed a little harder. "I'll call Oliver and see if he or one of his boys can park it a little better for—"

"—What's this I hear about a check?" Maxine asked, ignoring Myrtle's cavalier response to re-parking her car. "Did you get a check for that show?"

"You still haven't read that contract have you?"

"I didn't see anything that said anything about a check," Maxine replied annoyed.

"They sent us all a check," Myrtle explained. "I got one, but haven't deposited it. I'm still on the fence about this whole thing."

"How much was this check?"

"A thousand dollars," Myrtle replied. "I just might have to go on and deposit it," she chuckled. "…To get a dern mirror put back on the dern car!"

42

Maxine tore her house apart looking for this check. She wasn't like Mug, who had kids and grandkids living in the house, coming and going by key. She lived alone. If a check had been sent, then it was somewhere in the house. Like Myrtle, she could use a thousand dollars. She didn't need a mirror, but her car could use new tires. Also, her TV in the living room was on the fritz. The screen was so white that she only turned it on while she was in the kitchen cooking, listening to it like a radio. Plus, she needed to have her back door fixed. She no longer could use it, which made taking out the trash a pain in the behind. And she always could go for treating herself to a nice perfume, or maybe a necklace to go with the earrings Elaine bought.

But there was no check in the paper bins on her desk, or in any of the drawers, or space where she kept unopened bills. She looked in the kitchen trashcan, and checked old newspapers she kept by the fireplace. Nothing. She fanned out the magazines on her coffee table, and swiped a broom beneath her sofa, thinking maybe a stray piece of mail accidentally ended up there. Again, nothing. She snatched back the comforter on her bed. Sometimes she took mail upstairs and paid her bills there.

Eventually she picked up the phone and called Mug. "What did this check look like?"

"It was in a white envelope," Mug replied. "Mines was a green check. At first I thought it was one of them sweepstakes checks. You might've thrown it out."

That's what Maxine was afraid of, so she called Marsha,

the point of contact they were advised to call if they had questions, or changed their mind. Marsha put her on hold for a few minutes, before coming back on the line to tell her something that left her, for a change, speechless.

The check had already been cashed, what Marsha used to confirm which girls were participating in the interview.

"Well, I didn't cash that check," Maxine told Marsha.

"But are you now confirming that you will appear for the interview?"

"First I want to know who cashed that check because I never got it!"

"Well, I don't have that information in front of me, but can tell you where the check was sent and when and where it was cashed," Marsha replied, rattling off the correct mailing address and mentioning a date that immediately resonated with Maxine. It was just the other day! When her son had come over asking to borrow her car because his tags had expired. She told him hell no, not after his trifling wife couldn't pick her up from the airport.

"Let me call you back," she told Marsha.

Maybe her son accidentally picked up her mail, since he'd never stolen from her before. He wouldn't be alive, or in serious disrepair if he had. Never hit your momma or steal from her were her top deal-breakers.

"Naw Ma', I don't have none of your mail, but hang on, let me ask Phe," he said.

Maxine thought for a second. Why would he have to ask that damn Pheonix? She had no business in her house. And she definitely had no business looking through her mail. It took him a while to come back on the phone. And when he did, it wasn't him, but the wife.

"Umm...ummm," Phoenix started out hemming and hawing. "Umm, I might've cashed that check by accident," she got out.

It took everything she had not to drive over to Wister Street and rip her daughter-in-law's head right off her shoulders. She called Mug to help keep her out of jail. "How in the hell she gonna accidentally cash a check with my name on it!" she fumed.

"The real question is why she cashed a check with your name on it," Mug chuckled.

But Maxine wasn't in a laughing mood. "I'm on my way over to Wister Street, and she better hope and pray that bank gives me my money!"

It was by a major fluke that Maxine learned about the check 20 minutes after Phoenix had gone in the bank and cashed it. How she did it, Maxine didn't know, but was about to find out.

"I'm on my way," Mug said out one side of her mouth while calling for her daughter Debra out the other side.

"I need you to drop me off at Maxine's house," she explained, roughly resketching what Maxine told her. And yeah, it was only a block walk to Maxine's house, but she was too bone tired to walk that block, and wasn't interested in Maxine driving her anywhere in the frame of mind it sounded like she was in.

Debra though, trifling as she herself could be, thrived on tension. So she volunteered to drive them both, Mug and Maxine, over to Wister Street where her son lived with Phoenix.

"Y'all shouldn't be so hard on that girl," Debra said on the way over. "I feel sorry for her."

"You feel sorry for her," Maxine more like shrieked than asked. "Well, you're gonna feel sorrier for her if that bank don't have that check!"

"But Miss Maxine, you gotta really look at this whole thing."

"What do you mean!? I am looking at the whole thing! That heffa took a check with my name on it and—"

"—and she got it from Stevie," Debra said.

"Wha—What?" Maxine got quiet for a second. "But that don't matter, she—"

"—Naw Max, it does matter," Mug quietly replied, thinking about what her daughter was really saying. For as long as she had known Phoenix, and seeing her with Stevie, who at 42 remained as much a menace to society as he was at two, the girl fit every stereotype of weak women she'd seen coming through social services' doors. It was only easy to see Phoenix as a problem because she dressed a lot like a hooch, and talked tough...to everyone but Maxine of course. And yet, that girl was weak as ever, led and steered by none other than Stevie.

"Stevie knew about that girl cashing that check. I bet he even made her cash it," Mug said.

They got over to Wister Street and there standing out in the cold, dressed in a knit skirt hugging her wide hips, reaching nowhere near her knees, and shivering in a waist high thin jacket with her arms crossed, hugging herself to keep warm, was Phoenix all alone.

"Look at her," Maxine scoffed. "Pocketbook nowhere in sight! My momma always said never trust a heffa who don't carry a pocketbook!"

Phoenix climbed in the car and plopped down in the seat. Immediately Mug and Maxine gagged.

"Ooo!" Mug groaned, bringing a hand up to her mouth and covering her nose with two fingers as she cracked the window with her free hand.

"Good Lord," Maxine groaned too, looking over at Phoenix, giving her an evil eye. "You know you need to wash your ba'hind!"

Phoenix didn't say anything, but tried to pull the skirt over her knees.

"Why did you do this," Maxine asked. "That check had my name on it."

A tear fell from Phoenix's eye. "Stevie made me do it," she softly replied.

"Mmm umm," Mug sitting up front hummed. Just as she thought. She knew it, but kept quiet.

Turned out the bank couldn't return the check because Phoenix couldn't return the money. She didn't have it. Stevie had it. He drove Phoenix to a bank where one of his babies' mother worked and had the girl cash the check. The bank manager pulled the check from Stevie's baby's mama's teller drawer to find Maxine's name clearly on the front of the check, but Phoenix's signature and state ID number on the back.

"Ma'am, if they bring back the cash, I'll hold the check and give it to you when they do," the bank manager said.

Maxine got back on the phone and called Stevie. But he didn't answer. So they drove back to Wister Street, only to find her grandbabies, ages 2, 3 and 6 months, home alone and him gone.

"See, Stevie is wrong," Mug said. "To do that to his mother, and the mother of his children, he's the one that needs the ba'hind whipping!"

Maxine said nothing. Her hands stayed tightly clasped in her lap and her lips sealed shut. She hopped out of the car when Debra pulled up to her house and shut the door behind her, never saying another word about the incident.

Shirley called Mother and asked if she would drive Saturday morning, the day of the interview.

"I thought you didn't want to be bothered," Mother quipped.

"Chile, I don't tell y'all all my business," she chuckled, obviously in a good mood, because she rarely laughed.

The only reason Mother didn't challenge her on this, was because her girlfriend had been like this from the day they met, 46 years ago, seeming blessed with the best. Mother, like the other girls, looked up to Shirley for how together her life seemed, and not because she had a fine husband, the latest cars and the best household appliances. They believed her blessings came from not running her mouth, unlike them who everyone knew their business.

Like Myrtle who divorced her husband, after he made a mess of himself at one of her dinner parties. And of course Vera who's first husband ran off with her money, an account that actually made the front page of a local newspaper, in contrast to Maxine's ex-husband whose last meal was cherry pie, based on an autopsy done trying to find his cause of death. That event never made the papers, and the cause of death remained a mystery, speculation stayed on Maxine and a woman who used to live on Gorgas Lane, known for selling baked desserts. It was no secret, Mother had seen that woman leaving Maxine's house more than once when she wasn't home.

Interestingly enough, despite Mug and Oscar fighting like cats and dogs, and Mother and Joe rarely seen in the same place together, it was Mother and Mug who stayed married, and yet Shirley who the girls deeply respected.

Despite that one awful night when Chester tore doors off the hinges in their quiet home, and despite the girls' reluctance to credit Shirley for catching things that spared them extra grief, there was a humble strength in her silence. In Mother's eye, Shirley earned the right to get on her nerves.

"Well, I'm glad you called because I was starting to think it was just going to be me and Mug going."

"Unt un," Shirley smirked. "Max is going to be there, and so is Myrtle and Vera!"

Mother had her mouth open, but couldn't get words out. She was genuinely surprised. Vera sounded so absolute about not going, and so did Maxine. Usually when those two said they weren't doing something, they stuck to their word.

"Maxine's son cashed that check so now she has to go," Shirley laughed.

"What?"

"Yeah girl, Stevie had his girlfriend, I mean his wife cash that check and spent the money," she continued laughing. "Chile, Max was hot! Mug said Max almost beat the girl up."

So, that was Shirley, mum on her own business, but had no problem sharing other people's troubles.

"And I think Elaine's flying in tonight," Shirley went on. "She's supposed to be staying with Vera. That's why I think Vera is going. She could lie to us about that sick woman but couldn't lie to her girlfriend Elaine!"

"Oh girl, then we're going to have us a good time," Mother cheered. "I thought it was just going to be me and Mug."

Vera picked Elaine up at the Philadelphia International Airport just like Shirley said. Of course Shirley knew this because Vera called her first, asking if she could pick Elaine up. But Shirley told Vera she had plans. That was the night when she kicked up her feet to enjoy her empty nest watching back to back episodes of CHOPPED. Wasn't no way she was going to break that date, to sit in the house hosting Elaine for four days.

"In all these years this place still hasn't changed," Elaine said looking out the window as Vera drove over Platt Bridge and by the oil tanks, taking 76 to her home in Blue Bell. Had Vera looped around 95 to catch 476 instead, Elaine would've had a better view of the Comcast building, and most certainly would've noticed the new Lincoln Financial Field. She hardly would've missed the Eagles' stadium, one attraction that welcomed visitors to the city.

"When's the last time you've been home," Vera asked slightly annoyed.

"Oh no, this is no longer home for me," Elaine replied, smiling as she looked out the window. "Last time I've been here was the day I left... November 22, 1973, Thanksgiving Day. I was 27-years old."

Usually Vera would be cooing and wooing, showing off that swanky Southern bell in her flair. Entertaining hardwired in her DNA and indulging others flowing through her veins, this would have been a perfect spot to ask where she had gone on that Thanksgiving Day when she disappeared for twenty years.

For years the girls thought Elaine and her girls were in the Schuylkill, at the bottom of the river. And the only reason Ralph wasn't thrown in the river too, was due to him looking harder for Elaine than anyone. In a way, and an awfully awful view, but some hoped she was at the bottom of a river, or somewhere he could never find her. They certainly were reluctant to help him look.

Nonetheless, out of the many conversations Vera and Elaine had, this never came up. To hear them talk, no one would ever suspect a man as abusive as Ralph had been in their past. Mostly they regaled affluent affairs...billionaire pioneers and designers arranging private expos in Elaine's mansion, or Elaine hosting private parties for her network of friends, at a steep discount, also in Elaine's home. This was something the girls didn't know. Elaine's income derived from these private parties. It was how she afforded the mortgage. The few moments they had alone, were spent talking about their children, and offbeat soft incidentals such as vacation spots, food and the likes.

But Vera hadn't probed the private entails of Elaine's life before and wasn't about to do it then, though she struggled to impart the hospitality Elaine treated her to each time she visited Arizona. The bare truth was, she really didn't want to do the interview.

"Well, we certainly lost a lot of people, that's for sure," Vera replied pleasantly, less the usual fru-fru bells and whistles. "It's not as crowded as it used to be."

"To God be the glory," Elaine hummed, sounding as if in a far off dream. "Maybe it'll rid the city some of its filth."

"Ump," Vera wryly chuckled. "That's an interesting way to look at it."

"Do you remember all the kids in the neighborhood," Elaine suddenly asked, swinging around to look at Vera. "The neighborhood was just swathed in children!"

Vera smiled. Every house had at least three children, usually more sophisticated homes. Most had five, and it wasn't out of the ordinary to find ten or more children in the home.

"Yeah, I guess people aren't breeding like rabbits anymore," Vera sighed. "Young people today seem to have different values."

"Yeah, to stay away from dogs," Elaine scoffed.

"Ump," Vera softly huffed, trying to breathe, speak and keep her blood pressure in check. "Well, I haven't had the best luck at relationships, but surely don't see all men as dogs," she coolly replied, visualizing Sunday when Elaine would be headed back to where she could be pampered by eunuchs named Jorge, who served gourmet meals on her lovely veranda by the pool and was at her beckon call around the clock.

"I do," Elaine snipped. Her tone wasn't hostile but her words were clipped and curt. "Men are all the same, except maybe for their name!"

"So, I guess that's why you decided to do the interview," Vera gently pried. Annoyed as she was, Elaine had always been a gracious host whenever she visited. Maybe it was Arizona's crisp light air, or the eunuchs, or perhaps the hefty leasing fees she charged groups to pay her mortgage. Still, returning the hospitality was the least she could do.

"Actually, I was the one who suggested the interview," Elaine sprung on Vera. "One of my friends called one day, asking about the friends I left on Gorgas Lane," she explained. "She mentioned Shugga, something about the possibility of her being involved in foul play," she chuckled shaking her head.

"At any rate," she continued after a sigh, Vera's eye growing rounder and larger as Elaine's song played and played. "We talked and talked, me telling her about my friendship with Shugga, and her telling me about Mug..." and she paused. "Did you know Mug was held at gunpoint at her job?"

"Huh?" Vera had never heard about such an incident.

"Yeah, Mug is doing a lot for young women, why we thought to do a historical feature about sisterhood and women then and now. The city is going to honor Mug with a key to the city," Elaine said.

"Oh my goodness!" Vera shrieked. "Seriously!?!"

"Sssh!" Elaine chuckled. "Don't tell the girls. I only just heard about the key part. Initially it was—"

"—Oh Lord Elaine," Vera squealed, the bubbly side of her springing out. "Girl, I couldn't figure out what was going on. I wondered why you were calling out of the blue. Chile, you scared me to death," she sang on, relieved her weekend no longer would be billed with awkward chatter. "Oh my goodness, the girls are going to be so surprised. They're going to love this!"

46

Surprised as Vera was, and elated she could relax about having to anticipate underlying motives or clumsy chatter, she called Myrtle after getting Elaine set up in her guestroom.

"Mertie girl," she cooed in her lowest voice. "Did you buy that wig and them sunglasses you said you were getting," she playfully teased.

"I sure did," Myrtle belted. "Picked up a pair yesterday. Somebody might recognize me, but not everybody!"

"Girl, leave that mess at home," Vera chuckled. "Go on and wear the red suit. You don't want to be on national TV looking boo-boo the fool. I think we're going to have a ball!"

"Ump," Myrtle snorted, reaching for the Slims. "Well, I'm only going because you and Elaine are going."

"And because you cashed that check," Vera laughed.

"Ump," Myrtle snorted again. Each dog had its day. This was her day. "Yeah, well... it'll probably be better than catfighting with Sandy and them," she groused.

"Oh, what's going on with the Thetas," Vera cooed.

"Chile, one of our sorors wrote a book and is upset the Chapter isn't supporting it."

"Well, what's the book about?"

"I don't know what the book is about," Myrtle belted. "All I know is the president of the Chapter is talking about suspending that Chile!"

"Ooo, must've been an awful book," Vera cooed.

"Yeah, it was one of them self-published books she probably should've vetted," Myrtle replied. "You know how nowadays, everybody and their mama out here telling stories!"

"Well, I actually think we're going to have a good time," Vera said changing the subject.

"I hope you're right," Myrtle chuckled. "Last thing I need is to get suspended over some tell-all nonsense!"

"—But two days ago I thought you had returned that check and was going to your Chapter's Christmas party," Myrtle belted, switching the subject as well.

"No, that isn't this weekend," Vera said, pausing to think. "Wait, let me check my calendar," she said swiping at her phone. "…No, that's next weekend…Barry's party is this week…" she muttered, thinking out loud. "Oh Lord, I'ma have to call Barry and let him know I doubt I'll make that with Elaine here," she sighed.

"But what did you do with the check," Myrtle asked.

"I haven't done anything with it…yet." Vera replied. "I did call the people and told them I would participate though."

"So, what's Elaine's deal," Myrtle asked. "How'd she get roped up in this?"

"Mertie Girl, she's the one behind this show biz," Vera whispered.

"Lord! What!?" Myrtle shouted. "Wait a minute now… Elaine put this thing together!?"

Vera's grin hid her entire face. "Look, I don't know a thing," she chuckled. "But this isn't the half of it! The girls are in for a real surprise and treat!"

"Oh, so that's what the surprise talk was about…"

"You didn't hear it from me," Vera chuckled. She wasn't concerned about Myrtle picking up the phone and repeating their conversation, because one thing Myrtle wasn't, was a pot stirrer. She was loud, up front and had a voice like thunder, but she was like Ebenezer with a secret. In all the years they'd been friends, never once had she been found the center of controversary. They both were like this, avoiding duplicitous spotlights, even if she made one more phone call.

47

"Vaughn darling, it's Vera. I hate calling so late at night but I'm concerned about our girl."

Vaughn was Shugga's boss, the only man who saw more of Shugga and knew more about her than anyone on the face of the planet. This was a big deal, because no matter how little he knew, it would be more than all the girls combined.

"Oh, hi darling, you ain't bothering me," Vaughn coughed into the phone, sounding like he was sitting on his porch, drinking beer...and fishing. "What's up?"

Why Vera hadn't thought about contacting this man before, she considered it as she started to answer his question.

"Have you heard from my girl? We haven't seen her in a while."

"Well, no," he groused, sounding as if he was propping himself up by the elbows. "Last we talked she told me she'd be back after the first of the year. But I don't question Georgia. She tells me when she's coming to work. I just pay her," he chuckled.

"That's what we're hearing," Vera cooed. "But I was sending out my Christmas party invitations and didn't want her to accuse me of not inviting her."

"Are you sending me one," he teased. "I want to come."

"You know you're invited," Vera teased back. "You can come by and see me anytime," she openly put on, knowing Vaughn didn't know where she lived, unless he thought she lived at the Embassy Suites. And she might pass out and die of a heart attack if this man showed up at her door, dressed in lumber jack boots and wearing his usual two-week shadow. This was how he looked when they met at one of Shugga's

Christmas parties, an affair she didn't make the mistake attending twice.

One year many years ago, Shugga had sent her a gorgeous invitation, leading her to believe it was going to be a fabulous Christmas party. She personally called too, and begged her to come, telling her everybody would be there, which many attended, every one of them her scaffold co-worker buddies and their significant others, but no one Vera of course knew. Not any of the girls showed up. That's how Shugga was. Always up to something. She intentionally kept the party away from the girls, to tease them, fully anticipating Vera would later mention it, which she did, to her chagrin a day too late. It was hard to tell who really ended up the butt of the joke. Vaughn fell hard for her that evening, an affair, embarrassing as it was, that never truly ended. Vaughn was one secret she absolutely did not want to get out.

"Oh, wait," Vaughn said before their short flirty chat ended. "One of the guys may have talked to her recently. I heard them knuckleheads," and he paused to chuckle, "...well the guys have been laughing about the—ugh—ugh... you know," he stammered, leaving the sentence dangling there.

"Oh, come on darling," Vera teased. "You can tell your Vera what's going on with our Shugga," she laughed.

"Agh, well, you know..." Vaughn started stammering again, holding back on something that old-school men like him found embarrassing to talk about.

"No, I don't know," Vera cooed, smiling and wiggling her voice. "What are the boys teasing Shugga about?"

"Well...agh...well you know Georgia ain't the type to be with...agh...you know, Georgia ain't into men like that," he finally got out.

"Are you saying Shugga isn't interested in dating men?"

"No, I'm saying Georgia can't have sexual relations."

Silence. Complete silence canvassed the connection before Vera spoke. "Wait a minute, now. How do you know this Vaughn?"

"You mean Georgia hasn't told any of you she's closed up down there?" And Vaughn said this like common knowledge, as if he was Shugga's gynecologist.

Vera didn't miss a beat.

"Vaughn!" she shrieked. "Where in the devil did you hear this!? And how do you know!?"

"She told us, and I believe her," Vaughn replied, speaking just as flat and plain as black and white print in a book.

"Aww…Shugga was just pulling your legs," Vera chuckled. "She probably—"

"—Naw Veer," Vaughn said cutting her off, his voice steady and ascetic. "She explained how she was born with both genders. She said doctors cut off the wrong one because she has no female reproductive organs."

Vera listened, wondering out loud why Shugga would discuss such personal matters with co-workers, up on a scaffold, and not with her friends…and family!

That's when Vaughn got to chuckling again. "Look, you know how Georgia is. The guys were giving her a hard time one day and she just come out and said she was as much male as they were… and gosh be doggonit…she proved it too!"

"Oh Lord," Vera gasped, too drunk off this disclosure to say more.

"Yeah, that's why the guys have been in here cutting up, after hearing this stuff about her marrying some African."

48

"You ready!? I'm on my way over," Shirley chirped into the phone at the break of morning, hours before they had to be at the studio. She was not only dressed and had her hair in place, but she had had a sunny side up egg, a slice of toast and two cups of coffee.

But Mother wasn't ready. She was still in bed, feeling around for her glasses. It was by the grace of a divine force that she found the phone and hit the right button. So Shirley said she'd call back, which an hour later, after catching an episode of Joyce Meyer...the Christian missionary, and Judge Faith...the celebrity TV judge, she called again. Of course Mother wasn't ready then either. She was hanging over the sink, brushing her teeth. The ones in her hand, the first thing she did every morning. But she went on and fibbed anyway. "All I have to do is put on my clothes. But don't worry. You know Jenny will have us there in time!"

Shirley had no doubt, otherwise she would have drove herself, or rode with one of the other girls. But that's why she called ahead of time, because an hour and twenty minutes later she arrived at Mother's house to find her upstairs sitting on the bed, struggling to get her left leg in a pair of pantyhose.

"Girl, you still wear them things!"

"Chile, I have to," Mother panted. "I feel naked without them."

"That's why I wear pants," Shirley boasted. "That way I can put on some knee-hi's and be done with it."

"Chile, would you shut up and help me!" Mother laughed. "I can't bend down. Try to turn the toe around for me."

"What makes you think I can bend down," Shirley laughed. "If I get near that floor, you might have to call 911 to get me up off the floor too!"

"Girl, you ain't worth a quarter," Mother huffed, playfully of course. "Have you heard from Shugga? I keep hearing she is back in the states."

"Chile, Shugga been back," Shirley exclaimed. "She got back sometime last week, before we got back from Arizona."

"Why haven't you said anything!?"

"Girl, I already told y'all. I don't talk about my business. Besides, I don't know if she's here in the city yet. Last I heard, they were up there in New York, where they landed..." Shirley chuckled, tickled about something she knew, that no one else knew. "...Shugga talkin' about Cory wanted to see the city," she laughed, on a high when she had one up on everyone.

"In New York," Mother shrieked anyway. "Oh Lord, the girls—"

"—Yeah, apparently he claimed he couldn't see much sitting in a plane bent over," Shirley continued, talking over Mother. "He says he wants to meet Beyoncé and LeBron," she laughed.

"Beyoncé and LeBron," Mother huffed, looking up at Shirley like she was the crazy one. "What? He thinks Shugga knows them? Shugga don't know either one!"

"I know one thing," Shirley went on, "Shugga got that African up there in New York making the fool of the both of them," she said, cracking up laughing. "They rented a car and are staying at one of them cheap hotels in Jersey."

"Oh my goodness, then Shugga can drive down here at any time—"

"—Chile, Shugga done rented a convertible," Shirley said talking over Mother, shaking her head and well into the most humorous part of the story. "It's two degrees out and her simple ba'hind is riding around in a convertible so Cory can stretch his legs and sit up straight in the car..."

Mother fell out laughing. She had to use the bed to brace herself, to keep from falling and nicking her pantyhose.

"But that ain't it," Shirley continued. "They were going cross the bridge when the wig flew off!"

That time Mother fell on the bed, rocking back and forth she cried laughing so hard.

"Him and her got to fussing about going back to get the wig. Shugga said she lost it at the 45-mile marker," Shirley went on, laughing herself as she retold the story. "But you know what that traffic look like crossing the bridge into New York…it must've scared Cory to death.

Shugga said he wanted to buy her new hair, but you know how Shugga is about buying hair…she only get her hair from Mr. Kim," she chuckled, dragging out the story to both impress Mother with how much she knew, and humor her at Shugga's expense, something like killing three birds with one stone.

Mother howled and rolled. "Stop it Shirley! Stop it!" she cried laughing.

But Shirley kept going, on too much of a humor high to stop the story.

"Both of 'em was out there on the bridge, the African asking her how she knew where 'da ting flew off to, and her telling him 'da ting flew off at the 45-mile marker because that's where she felt it coming loose."

"Shirley no, stop it," Mother laughed, tears streaming over her face. "When did you talk to Shugga? When did she tell you all this?"

"Chile, she called me last night, asking if her and Cory can stay with me…her pipes at the house froze up, plus she wanted to know if I still had any of Mattie's wigs."

Abruptly Mother stopped laughing, and her mouth and eyes dropped. "You mean to tell me Shugga is here," she whispered, though not trying to keep anyone from overhearing them. In her line of reasoning, Shugga had to be in the city if she knew her pipes were frozen.

Mother shook her head vigorously, talking as she rushed into the bathroom to freshen up her make-up, and rushed into her closet to shuffle through hangers looking for the gold sequin jacket her middle daughter bought for the occasion.

"Chile, I can't wait to see Shugga…Lord I hope she found some hair… or a hat at least…"

"Well, you better hurry up before they lock the doors," Shirley said, just as excited, though excited for other reasons.

She hated being on colored people's time, no matter what the event.

"All I have to do is grab some tissues," Mother said panting as she hurried into her new jacket.

"I just want to get on the road," Shirley said, getting antsy about the drive as usual. "The crazies are going to be up in a minute. We don't want to get stuck behind a crazy getting over Broad Street."

"Girl, you know I don't take the nigga route," Mother chuckled grabbing her purse and roughly rousing through it looking for Jenny's keys. "There's a hundred ways to get over there. I'm taking Stenton Ave!"

"Stenton Ave," Shirley questioned. "But you'll be going way out of the way."

What a silly thing to say. "Girl, you just hold on to your wig," Mother teased, though Shirley didn't wear one, and never did. "Me and Jenny got this! We're gonna have you there in no time. You're gonna feel like you're flying the friendly skies!"

49

But not that time. Jenny didn't come through that time. By the time Mother and Shirley arrived at the TV studio, everyone was there. Myrtle. Maxine. Mug. Vera. And Elaine. They weren't first, and almost were locked out, as stipulated in the contract what would happen once the interview was in progress.

The two walked in and got the girls started right away.

"Aww, Lord! Here comes trouble and double trouble," Myrtle belted, holding center court dressed in a virgin wool red dress suit, standing out like Santa Claus on the 4th of July.

Right away Shirley rolled her eyes. She wanted to be seated in a corner, quietly watching and taking notes, a habit she picked up from her mother who used to lament, "the early bird gets the worm, that's why black folk don't have nothing… always running on their time!"

But that didn't happen, thanks to her girlfriend looking like a knockoff Patti LaBelle taking Stenton Ave.

"Y'all haven't miss nothing," Mug chuckled, herself looking like a goddess Buddha sent. She was wrapped in a bulk of shiny gold fabric, and layers of it, head to toe. The head-wrap, about fifty pounds of taffeta fabric, she had tied in a series of twists, coils and knots. The dress, made up of a skirt and shawl, covered her from the neck down to a half inch above her ankles. Again, she was elaborately draped in the fabric, reminiscent of the African characters in the movie Coming to America. And on her feet were gold shoes she picked up on Ridge Avenue, about the only place to find shoes that less than two or three people in the world had a pair.

"Yes, we're about to head to the green room," Marsha said, flanked by Rita, the KYL executive producer, and a smiling ear-to-ear little man she introduced as Richard Gordon. "He's our production assistant," she explained. "He's going to take care of you guys while you're in the green room."

"Well, come on now," Mother cackled, snapping her fingers, ready to get the party started. "I want to meet everyone, including the big boss" she laughed, everything on her, from the glossy red lipstick to the costume jewels shimmering and glistening. "…In case we have to sue somebody for misquoting us," she added.

Shirley rolled her eyes again and made her way behind Vera cheesing the girth of the Atlantic, dialed up a notch above Myrtle, wearing a premier designer off the shoulder long poofy sleeve African print dress, with a deeply bold neckline, high waist, and slit that started at the calf and ended at the fleshiest part of her thigh. The dress was a knockout, leaving nothing to the imagination, though very little skin showed.

"I'm Rita Shivers," said the woman flanking Marsha, uncrossing her arms and stepping forward to shake Mother's hand. "I'm the executive producer for KYL."

"Meaning she's going to be the one who you'll be speaking to if you get to running off at the mouth," Maxine teased.

"Aww shucks now, a head woman in charge," Mother grinned ignoring Maxine, shaking the woman's hand like she wanted to keep it for a souvenir.

"Alright Ladies," Marsha said clapping her hands, cutting the awkward interruption in half. "Let's head on over to the green room so we can get started."

The girls adjusted themselves, Mug patting the fifty-pound bulk of fabric on her head, and Vera slipping her von Furstenberg clutch beneath her arm, and followed Marsha.

"Now, to give you the heads up," Marsha continued, talking and walking, "this is going to be a very informal chat. So, there's no need to worry about censoring what you say because we aren't going to be live."

"Good," Myrtle chuckled, "they'll probably end up with about five minutes of usable tape."

"Well, I don't want nothing I say cut," Mug scoffed. "Let me find out I got cut, and I'll be doing some cutting of my own!"

The girls laughed, but not as raucous as usual. They were a little out of their element and needed time to warm up.

"Yeah, we aren't exactly known for biting our tongues," Mother added. "Hope this show is properly rated!"

"And that's just how we want you all to be," Marsha replied. "Viewers love reality!"

"And druggies love heroin and cocaine too," Maxine muttered.

"We'll be editing the interview anyway, so..." Marsha continued before stopping mid-sentence to turn to Richard. "Did you happen to find that extra microphone?"

Maxine stopped dead in her tracks, causing Myrtle to bump into her. "Wait a minute—" she started, interrupted by Myrtle.

"—Chile, take it out on Stevie's ba'hind when you get home," she muttered teasing.

"She already did," Mug chuckled. "She beat about ten times the amount of that check out of that boy."

Mother burst out laughing, causing Elaine to jump and Vera to spin around, graciously of course.

"Max Guurrl..." Vera cooed. "I want you sitting right beside me," and she squealed, "so the world can see when we come out of the house, we don't play!"

"Yeah, that is a bad jacket," Elaine said.

Maxine, dressed like Max, wore a soft butterscotch leather jacket, with her signature stenciled in the fabric, nothing that came from the slender budget her son had stolen from her. This jacket was made during a trip she'd taken to Spain, by an apprentice she met in a side alley peddling his designs.

In the green room, which wasn't so much green as it was white, Marsha and Rita disappeared, leaving the girls with little Richard...no pun intended...to point out the restrooms and refreshments, and answer any questions they had.

"So, how long have you been here Richard," Mother asked.

"Oh, you can call me Rich," he politely said, breaking his wrist as he talked. "I've been here three years today, but—"

"—Three years," Mother shrieked. "Chile, you look like you were three, ten years ago!"

"Oh, you're so kind," Richard schmoozed. "It must be the height thing, huh?"

"Actually no. It's the wrist thing," Mother chuckled.

"Oh...oh..." Richard replied, clumsily catching on.

"Well, happy annivers—" Myrtle started to belt, cut off by Vera's whine.

"—Richey darling, would you be a doll and see if someone can do something about the temperature," she said batting her lashes and fanning herself. "I'm having a moment and don't want to hinder any of our plans."

"Girl, are you sure that's a moment and not Christ coming for you," Mother teased as Richard hurried out of the room. "Oh Lord! Jesus Christ!" Myrtle belted, all heads swinging her way, all except for Elaine quietly inspecting photos of past guests memorialized on the walls.

The same one thought registered on each of the girl's faces. Where is she...and he?

"What in the devil did I just put in my mouth," Myrtle fussed, spitting into a napkin.

Aside from Mug who covered her mouth to laugh, and Maxine who glared at Myrtle like she was about to pull the chiffon scarf around her neck extra tight, Shirley elbowed Mother and muttered in her ear. "Don't you open your mouth!"

"I might have to send Rich over to Joe's Crab Shack when he gets back here," Myrtle said, oblivious to the stir she caused. "I've had quiche before, but that ain't quiche!"

50

Richard whizzed back in the room, smiling and waving at Vera as if seeing her for the first time.

"Ms. Vera, we fixed the circulation issue... do you feel better," he asked, looking directly into her dark eyes with his pebble-sized blue eyes.

"Darling, you're a miracle worker," Vera replied. "I feel just wonderful!"

"Well, Ladies," Richard said, spinning in a semi-circle to be sure he made eye contact with each of them. "We're about ready...did everyone get something to munch on...and find the facilities okay? Is there anything ...oh," he said interrupting himself. "I almost forgot."

The girls shifted but kept quiet, amused by Richard's upbeat flair. He wasn't big as a minute but had a personality almost as big as theirs. He had their full attention, seeming to have performed his routine many times before.

Looking down at the pad in his hand he started flipping pages. "Okay, so we received questionnaires back from only three of you...Ms. Catherine, Julia and Shirley..." he read off the pad, flipping pages back and forth before looking up. "But the script editor needs the occupation of everyone who didn't send back the questionnaire," he said.

"Now Richey, what's this for," Vera cooed.

"Well, it's so that when each of you speak, it displays in the caption," he replied.

"Then put the rest of us down as retired," Myrtle wryly chuckled. "I don't need nobody knowing how to find me. I have enough drama to deal with."

"Umm..." Richard stammered, not wanting to offend

the girls, but clearly Myrtle's fix wasn't going to work.

"Why don't y'all just say retired teacher, or education or something," Shirley spoke up.

"Yes Shirley, that is right," Vera sarcastically replied, switching her tone to address Richard. "I'm a retired house-wife," she cooed.

Myrtle and Maxine replied similarly. Myrtle a retired teacher, and Maxine a retired store clerk. Richard quickly jotted down their responses and flipped the pad over about to move on to where he was when Maxine interrupted him.

"You forgot one," she said.

"Ooo," and he returned to flipping the pages looking for the oversight before Myrtle uncrossed her legs at the ankles and looked around the room.

"Elaine Girl, are you retired too, or are you still doing the soap operas," she chuckled.

Richard wrinkled his forehead. "Umm...but..."

"Hi Richard," Elaine softly replied, raising her hand and twinkling her fingers.

"Oh my God girl," Richard shrieked, hesitating and stumbling over his words. "I didn't even recognize—umm—I thought..."

"...It must be the boots," Elaine teased, sparing him the trouble of explaining. "I usually start from the head, and not the other way around," she chuckled, imparting an inside joke only those in high-end fashion caught.

"Well, you look fabulous," Richard grinned, looking at her in a way he hadn't admired the other girls. He had checked them out, from head to toe without much comment. With Elaine he didn't so much as glance at anything she wore, despite the boss leather Moschino dress fitting every curve, and to include the Jimmy Choo ankle boots.

She embraced him warmly, whispering in his ear. "Looks like we have the green light."

Quickly she stepped back and for the girls' benefit, watching closely, she coolly replied, "it's such a small world. Rich and I go back to my early days in the business."

Vera looked down and noticed a piece of lint on her dress. Mug and Maxine exchanged a look.

And Shirley muttered to Mother, "here we go..."

Richard tucked the pad beneath his arm and clapped his hands. "Alright, chop! Chop! Looks like we've got the green light!

"Lord! Where's my shades," Myrtle belted digging in her purse.

"Girl no," Vera said tapping Myrtle's hand. "We won't be needing any shades. We're walking out on that set showing the same class we walked in here with. There are some young people out there counting on us painted cats."

The Creed of Painted Cats

They are the Mother's, and Myrtle's, and Shirley's
They are the Elaine's, the Mug's, and the Vera's
They are the Maxine's and they are the Shugga's too
Women who embrace their inherent distinct attributes,
curves, boobs, onset of the menses
desire to love and be loved
to date, marry,
and move on when things aren't right
the ability to birth new life
for those with reproductive types.
They are truth-sayers and naysayers.
Veils, nails, jewels, and purses
They are nurturers, worshippers,
on occasion ba'hind whippers
They'll lift you up, like they'll sit you down
will put it on the table
and keep it under the table
Telling it like it is giving you the bizz
IAMHER comes with her décor
From the bedroom to boardroom
They aren't always right.
Sometimes they make mistakes.
Where one is weak, the other strong.
Throw in menopause, and a whole lot of gossip,
plus the ability to be real, and keep it real,
unfurls a human flawed
no less proud homemakers
rare painted cats
real movers and shakers.

Other Books *by the* Author

Memoirs

Black Table
God Be the Glory
****NEW Babies Raising Babies*

Novels (Series)

Leiatra's Rhapsody (I)
Something Xtra Wild (II)
This One I Got Right (III)
Rye n the Rump (IV)
My Love (V)

Other Fiction

Pretty Inside Out
A Piece of Peace
Tehuelche
Pleasure
Double Dare
Lock Box
Big Bully
Copy Cats
Mindless

Short Stories

My Blackberry
Storytella

Poetry

Atlóta
GEM
A Blast From the Past
Civil Talk

RYCJ is a book reviewer, blogger, publisher, and storyteller. Since 2009 she has written dozens of books in a mosiac of genres, and has read and reviewed hundreds of books. She is the ultimate book lover, passionate about reading and writing stories that educates, entertains and inspires.